Publisher: Sinister Wisdom, Inc.
Editor: L.B. Johnston & Julie R. Enszer
Associate Editor: Amy Hong
Graphic Designer: Nieves Guerra
Copy Editor: Amy Hong
Board of Directors: Roberta Arnold, Tara Shea Burke, Cheryl Clarke, Julie R. Enszer, Sara Gregory, J.P. Howard, Joan Nestle, Mecca Jamilah Sullivan, Yasmin Tambiah, and Red Washburn

Cover Art: *Erasers No. 1* - **Artist:** Lisa Congdon
Media: Photograph
Size of artwork: 11x14 inches

Artist Biography: Illustrator and author Lisa Congdon is best known for her colorful, graphic drawings and hand lettering. She works for clients around the world including Comme des Garçons, Crate and Barrel, Facebook, MoMA, REI, and Harvard University among many others. She is the author of eight books, including the starving-artist-myth-smashing *Art Inc: The Essential Guide to Building Your Career as an Artist* and her latest book *Find Your Artistic Voice: The Essential Guide to Working Your Creative Magic* (August 2019). She was named one of 40 Women Over 40 in 2015 and she is featured in the 2017 book, *200 Women Who Will Change the Way You See the World*. She lives and works in Portland, Oregon.

Artist Statement: I am a self-taught painter and photographer. When I began making art twenty years ago in my early thirties, I found an expression for my interior world, and this experience profoundly transformed my relationship to my own grief and struggle as a queer person and a woman. I was, at the time, confronting years of intense depression, and art became a tangible way for me to express what was stuffed deep inside of me. Initially, I had no aspirations to become a professional artist; when I discovered the creative process, I simply wanted to be engaged in it all of the time because it brought me a sense of purpose and happiness that I had previously never felt. My work has matured over the past twenty years, mostly as a result the evolution that happens when an artist creates a lot of work. Because I wasn't formally trained, I learned to paint and draw and take photographs by experimentation – trying techniques over and over until I got them right. I began sharing my work on the Internet several years after I started making art. From there, my professional career began when I began getting inquiries from clients interested in hiring me to do illustration and from galleries and collectors.

Many of my paintings and photographs are arrangements of objects, both real and imagined. When I was a child, I began collecting things, and by the time I was in my twenties, I was spending weekends perusing flea markets and antique malls looking for small treasures. Simultaneously, from the time I was about eight years old, I developed an interest in arranging and displaying my collections. In hindsight, I realize that my need to collect and arrange were born of the need to both find comfort and create order in a world that felt unwieldy and out of control. My interest in arranging things neatly, even in my abstract paintings, has been a consistent theme in my work since I began painting and drawing. My paintings often elevate mundane, ubiquitous, sometimes obsolete objects into conversation with symbols from nature and the supernatural. I am particularly interested in eliminating complexity and detail in my subject matter, and in stripping things down to their essential forms.

My photographs of arrangements take mundane everyday objects (mostly vintage office & school supplies) and organize them by color and like objects. I enjoy the experience of taking everyday objects that might seem boring on their own (old erasers, bread tags, boxes of staples, matches) and creating beautiful, textured visual imagery by clustering those objects together on an imaginary grid and photographing them from above on a stark, white background. In 2010, I made such arrangements every day for an entire year (mostly photographed, some drawn) in a personal project called "A Collection a Day". The popularity of the images in that daily project was astonishing— the project was written about in *Martha Stewart Living*, *The Atlantic Magazine* and *The New York Times Magazine*. This intensive year of documenting collections also renewed my interest in type and packaging, since much of what I collect and photograph are old erasers, boxes of pencil leads, and other vintage office supplies. I realized that the popularity of the project was partly due to the attraction viewers had to the organization of the objects. But part of the attraction was that the objects evoked nostalgia. So many of the things in my arrangements were old, things we grew up using in school or watched our mom or grandma use while mending our clothes. Similar to the feelings that come with opening a box from your childhood and smelling the old, musty paper, viewing photographs of old things also fills us with lively, sometimes visceral memories.

Back Cover Art: *Dance Club* - **Artist:** Pamela Dodds
Media: Oil on Canvas
Size of artwork: 78 inches x 78 inches

Artist Biography: Pamela Dodds's visual art practice in painting, drawing, and printmaking explores the complexities of our human relationships, engaging with and exploring the inter-connectedness of humanity across time and space, with a focus on women and women's agency. Her work has been exhibited in the USA, Canada, and most recently in Europe, including at Lesbian ARTivisms Colloquium, University of Ottawa, Canada (2016), FiLiA Feminist Conference, London, UK (2017), and solo and group exhibitions in Spain, Finland, Cleveland, Ohio and Toronto. Collectors include Purdue University, Carleton University, Boston Public Library, Cleveland Museum of Art, and many individuals. To see images of her work, to purchase work, or propose an exhibition, please visit her website at www.pameladodds.net

SINISTER WISDOM, founded 1976
Former editors and publishers:
Harriet Ellenberger (aka Desmoines) and Catherine Nicholson (1976–1981)
Michelle Cliff and Adrienne Rich (1981–1983)
Michaele Uccella (1983–1984)
Melanie Kaye/Kantrowitz (1983–1987)
Elana Dykewomon (1987–1994)
Caryatis Cardea (1991–1994)
Akiba Onada-Sikwoia (1995–1997)
Margo Mercedes Rivera-Weiss (1997–2000)
Fran Day (2004-2010)
Julie R. Enszer & Merry Gangemi (2010–2013)
Julie R. Enszer (2013–)

Copyright © 2019 *Sinister Wisdom*, Inc.
All rights revert to individual authors and artists upon publication.
Printed in the U. S. on recycled paper.

Subscribe online: www.SinisterWisdom.org
Join *Sinister Wisdom* on Facebook: www.Facebook.com/SinisterWisdom
Follow *Sinister Wisdom* on Instagram: www.Instagram.com/sinister_wisdom
Sinister Wisdom is a US non-profit organization; donations to support the work and distribution of *Sinister Wisdom* are welcome and appreciated. Consider including *Sinister Wisdom* in your will.

Sinister Wisdom, *2333 McIntosh Road, Dover, FL 33527-5980 USA*

TABLE OF CONTENTS

Notes for a Magazine 7
MOLLY MARTIN
    What Old Tradeswomen Talk About 10
JONI RENEE WHITWORTH
    Inherent Wickedness 14
KRISTY LIN BILLUNI
    Not That Kind of Teacher: Inspiration and Instruction
        at the Crossroads of Writing and Sex 18
ASHLEY TREBISACCI
    What We Share 25
SHIVANI DAVÉ
    protect your femme 32
JILLIAN ETHERIDGE
    Away Game 33
JAY WHITTAKER
    Local Knowledge 43
ROBIN REAGLER
    Nothing Rattles the DJ 44
MO FOWLER
    Slack 45
JENNIFER ABOD
    Ash Wednesday 53
AMY LAUREN
    Miz Gill 55
SUZANNE FELDMAN
    There I Was in Art School 56
SB SŌWBEL
    Learning on the Job 64
ELIZABETH GALOOZIS
    Memorial Hill 65
    The Branches Regard the Tree 67
SARAH PRITCHARD
    Guitar Woman 68
SHELONDA MONTGOMERY
    Sunday Morning 69

GLORIA KEELEY
    Billie 83
    Janis Joplin, We Miss You 84
WENDY JUDITH CUTLER
    I (Still) Want a Women's (and Lesbian Feminist) Revolution .. 86
YVONNE ZIPTER
    Lighter Than Air 92
    True Love 94
OLIVIA SWASEY
    Old Friends 95
NATALIE ELEANOR PATTERSON
    Penelope's Vision 101
    Love Poem Sans Passion 102
FALLEN KITTIE
    Borders of Salt 103
BETH BROWN PRESTON
    Descant 109
CLAUDIA LARS (TRANSLATED BY BETH BROWN PRESTON)
    Sketch of a Frontier Woman 110
GABRIELA MISTRAL (TRANSLATED BY BETH BROWN PRESTON)
    God So Wills 112
JESSICA LOWELL MASON
    Wild Nights — Lesbian Lives!
        The Emily Dickinson Homestead, Revisited 114
SAMIRA NEGROUCHE (TRANSLATED BY MARILYN HACKER)
    Variations on a Minor Third 119

    Letters 124
    Interviews With Merril Mushroom About Her Play Bar Dykes .. 132

    Book Reviews 139
    Janice Gould — A Remembrance 159
    Janice Gould Bibliography 173

    Snapshot Lesbian Love Celebration 176

    Contributors 179

NOTES FOR A MAGAZINE

When LB Johnston approached me about a special issue of the journal on the subject of Lesbian Learning, I was intrigued by the idea. What do lesbians learn from one another? How do we learn from each other? What is the role of learning in our lives? The material that came together in this issue is excellent; I am excited to share it with you as *Sinister Wisdom* 115: *Lesbian Learning*.

While compiling this issue and working it through production, I thought about the various generational elements of lesbian learning. The patriarchal model is that children learn from elders. There is truth and value in that model; children do learn from elders and there is much for children to learn—and for young people to learn from people who are older than them. A fundamental insight of feminism, however, is that the patriarchal models do not tell us the full story. Learning is a reciprocal, life-long process. Elders learn from young people who bring new experiences and new knowledges to us all. Learning is multifaceted and continuous; all of us at every different age learn together and from one another. *Sinister Wisdom* 115: *Lesbian Learning* embraces this feminist insight and brings together voices that invite us to think, learn, and grow together.

I applaud LB's vision for this issue and her work to make it happen. It has been a pleasure to see this issue come to life and bring so many new and vibrant voices to the pages of *Sinister Wisdom*. I hope you enjoy reading it as much as I have enjoyed working on it.

In the late spring of 2019, we learned that *Sinister Wisdom* was a finalist for a Firecracker Award. The Firecracker Awards for Independently Published Literature "celebrate books and magazines that make a sparkling contribution to our literary culture and the publishers that strive to introduce important voices to readers far and wide." The awards are given by the Community of

Literary Magazines and Publishers (CLMP). I have submitted all of the issues of the journal each year for the awards. In part, I want to support CLMP, which is an important advocacy organization for the small press community; but I also believe in the excellence of our publishing, and I believe that it is as excellent as many of the other august literary magazines that are recognized each year. This year, *Sinister Wisdom* was a finalist. I was thrilled and deeply honored.

Being recognized as a finalist puts *Sinister Wisdom* in a longer and larger conversation with feminist publishers and the independent publishing organization. In 1979, CCLM (the Coordinating Council of Literary Magazines, the predecessor organization of CLMP) awarded an editor fellowship to the iconic lesbian-feminist journal *Conditions*. In a letter to readers of *Conditions*, the three editors, Elly Bulkin, Jan Clausen, and Rima Shore, noted that the "feminist protest following the announcement of the 1979 awards no doubt had an impact on the decision-making process." The first round of editor fellowships were awarded to all men; Maureen Owen, the only woman on the CCLM board of directors, received appeals from Adrienne Rich and Ellen Marie Bissert demanding change. For the *Conditions* editors, the award "represents the only substantial payment we have received, or seem likely to receive, for our editorial work, and we were greatly encouraged by it." Owen acknowledged the importance of the protests saying, they "strengthened my position on the board at CCLM and the position of women editors and writers in general. She who shouts, get heard!"

Forty years later, *Sinister Wisdom* echoes these sentiments, and appreciates this acknowledgement of our work from the community of independent publishers. Owen's words remain true: "She who shouts, gets heard!" Women, lesbians, and other marginalized voices shout to be heard; we also whisper and sing and write and publish. *Sinister Wisdom* is pleased to be a part of this literary community, thrilled to be recognized—in such amazing company—as one of the ten finalists, and honored to receive this award.

Thank you all for helping to keep *Sinister Wisdom* a vibrant and on-going lesbian literary and art journal.

In sisterhood,

Julie R. Enszer
January 2020

WHAT OLD TRADESWOMEN TALK ABOUT

Molly Martin

My friend Marg was building a coffin for her friend Bob. Marg was happy and excited that she could give back in this way, being a carpenter. But her project plans had to take into account her disability, a persistent back pain that had put an end to her career as a building inspector and that she now spends her life managing.

When we get together Marg and I often collaborate on inventions and engineer projects that never get built. But now she was actually completing one of them.

The funeral home had given Marg the dimensions of the concrete box that the coffin would have to fit into with the admonition that another coffin builder had exceeded the dimensions and at the burial the coffin had not fit.

At lunch with our retired carpenter friend Pat, Marg described her plan—a rectangular box rather than the typical hexagonal coffin shape. She used one four-by-eight sheet of plywood ripped in half lengthwise for the sides and ends. Another ripped sheet made the bottom and top. She made the handles with rope.

"I had the lumberyard rip the ply for me, to save my back," said Marg. "I can still use a Skil saw to crosscut short lengths, but I don't do ripping anymore."

She screwed a ledger around the inside of the box so the bottom could just be dropped in and sit on the ledger. I'm an electrician, not a skilled carpenter, so I was proud of myself for knowing that a ledger is the ribbon of wood attached to the framing of a wall that the floor hangs on. I could totally visualize it.

"What size plywood are you using?" asked Pat.

"Half inch," said Marg.

"Cross bracing?" asked Pat.

"Well, no," said Marg. "I don't think it needs it. I used structural plywood. Anyway, the coffin is now at the funeral home."

Pat and I looked at each other and each knew what the other was thinking. I imagined the bottom piece of plywood bending with the weight of Bob's body, the ply slipping off the ledger and the bottom piece along with the body falling out the bottom of the coffin as it was lifted up.

A moment of collective panic ensued. Marg frowned. She is a worrier.

"I'm sure it will be fine," said Pat.

Marg's description of her liberal use of glue and screws eased my concern.

Marg says there have been great strides made lately in screw technology. Hex head screws that go in easily, and you don't have to pre-drill.

"Oh My Goddess! Remember when we didn't have battery-operated drills?" I said. "I had to reach into my tool belt for a hammer and an awl to start the hole, and then screw in the screw with an old-fashioned slotted head screwdriver. In those days we used three-quarters-inch sheet metal screws to strap our electrical pipe to the wall. I had awesome forearms. People noticed my forearms."

"Yeah, I had an awesome back till I fell off that ladder," said Marg.

"And my knees were once awesome," said Pat, who was recovering slowly from a recent knee replacement.

We were just generally awesome.

Pat Cull, carpenter, measures twice

Marg Hall Marching at the 2017 Women's March in Oakland, California

INHERENT WICKEDNESS
Joni Renee Whitworth

I woke up most winter mornings of 1999 in faded flannel sheets, sandwiched between my dad and Blaze, our elderly Doberman. The alarm went off at 5:15 a.m., but we usually snoozed it a few times due to the cold: a pervasive, wet Oregon chill that breezed through our 1880s Yamhill County farmhouse and left a dewy sheen on the wallpaper. Blaze, Dad, and I had to share space because of the cold and lack of central heat, but also because of the sadness. Mom had left us about a year prior on account of my inherent wickedness. She'd been threatening to leave if the rain, the neighbors, and the three of us didn't start acting right.

I can't recall now what acting right would have entailed, but clearly none of us did it because in October of '98, after a Girl Scout Juniors troop meeting in the basement of a church whose God never spoke, Mom told me she was going to make a new life for herself in California. She got an apartment near Disneyland and rarely looked back. It rained from October to June.

Dad and I didn't have an easy way with words. We made up for what we couldn't voice about the sadness with snuggling. We'd wander the house at night wearing four or five layers each, sipping on a piping hot calcium-magnesium drink that was supposed to ward off nightmares. Then we'd slip under massive piles of quilts and hold each other and Blaze until dawn. To this day I feel an urge to cuddle, a desire to find comfort in the arms of a manager giving me feedback, a flight attendant handing me a ginger ale, a grocery store clerk reminding me that quinces are not in season.

In those days, breakfast was a harried affair of puffed rice with skim milk before heading out the door. We drove over backcountry roads dusted with frost, past filbert orchards and nurseries that grew starter trees for The Home Depot. After half an hour we'd arrive at our carpool drop-off point, which was the house of my older classmate and friend, Emma. She lived in an A-frame home on the way to our school. Emma had two parents, central heat, and a rescued husky/shepherd mix, who would howl wildly whenever my dad's tires crunched over their driveway gravel. This was Emma's signal to wake up and run down to unlock the front door for me. I'd hug my dad goodbye, dash through the rain, squeeze through the front door, and throw my wet backpack and raincoat on the entryway floor. The house was always still dark at that time, and Emma's parents would be asleep. My dad would wave and pull away to drive ninety minutes to a bookkeeping job in Portland.

Emma's home was blissfully warm. I'd doze on the entryway sofa for an hour or so while her family tromped around the house, waking up, making eggs over easy with thick slabs of succulent ham, Folger's coffee, and orange juice from a freezer can. Her family seemed very rich to me, but in retrospect, we were all teetering on the highest rung of the lowest class.

Emma's mom was a harsh and unsympathetic figure who mostly relegated me to the sofa while they enjoyed private family time, which meant breakfast, before we clambered into their van and carpooled the remaining thirty minutes to school. She did, however, permit Emma to make me a cup of chamomile tea before we left each morning. Perhaps you've had chamomile tea before—often recommended for colds and flus, fragrant, inexpensive, easily found, and enjoyed around the world. I wish you could try Emma's chamomile tea.

She'd start by carefully filling a porcelain china cup a sliver past half-full with scalding water. Then she'd add one tea bag from a giant bulk box and wait beside me while the tea cooled. She didn't touch me much. I felt our upper arms resting together as we watched the tea steep, or she'd brush a passing hand by my back, but she felt like a thousand fireplaces: a melting that reached into my inner places. She'd heap in spoonfuls of brown sugar and stir slowly, until the water had dissolved every crystal. To this, she'd add a dash of heavy cream.

When I think about being gay, I don't pathologize my coming-of-age narrative or turn to Lady Gaga for a "born this way" anthem. Instead, I wonder if my path to queerness was laid in the quiet and in-between moments. I loved Emma. I loved her tea. Simple. This was before I learned about the gender binary, femme ritual, sandal brands, derby daddies, bathhouse etiquette, goddess worship—all the theory and culture that came later and perhaps only complicated my senses. My feelings for Emma were too serene to be lust, too embodied to be theoretical. She served that tea to me with half a slice of rye toast every school day. Y2K came and went.

In July, we learned that the bookstore down the lane from where Emma lived was planning an elaborate midnight release party for *Harry Potter and the Goblet of Fire*. We eagerly counted down the days. When the evening of the party came, we dressed up like witches and waited, cross-legged, on the faded blue carpeted floor of the bookstore, listening to the excited whispers of a hundred witches and warlocks. We all screamed when midnight struck. The bookstore employees wheeled out towering carts of wrapped books, which we grabbed and began to read immediately, shushing the bad, noisy children aside us. We stayed up furiously reading until almost everyone had gone home, and a reporter took our picture for the *News-Register*, the community newspaper of the Willamette Valley.

Summer in the new millennium felt bolder. Peonies and blooming lilac trees dotted our potholed roads, which I could skip down all day since school was out. Blaze started sleeping outside, guarding the farmhouse. Dad was away a lot, either because of work or the sadness. Maybe it was the heat or the alone time that emboldened me, or maybe it was inherent wickedness, but that summer I took a neighbor girl to my hot attic and kissed her on the mouth. I pulled down her cotton underpants and watched as she pulled down mine, and as neither of us knew what happened next, we stayed that way for hours, kissing, cuddling, sweating.

What did happen next was a grand dichotomy: moments of terror and beauty, more than any one thing or the sum of some rapid harvests. In the season of the mustard bloom, vintners came with out-of-state money, and the gravel roads all got paved. My blueberry pie took third place at the fair, and the neighbor girl's stepdad died of an opioid overdose, as many local parents did. The valley got a beautiful new bypass; traffic's down by forty percent. I took a job pouring wine for tourists, and Emma moved to Denver, where she eventually married an electrician who is successful and emotionally abusive to her. All the Harry Potter books, then the films, were released to great critical acclaim. Now, in the quiet and in-between moments, I search online for tips and tricks on how to spread a father's ashes, for rescue dogs, and for women on Tinder. I explain to them that touch is more than a love language. It is my native language.

NOT THAT KIND OF TEACHER: INSPIRATION AND INSTRUCTION AT THE CROSSROADS OF WRITING AND SEX

Kristy Lin Billuni

"Sister, when you get, give. When you learn, teach."
—Maya Angelou

"What are you ashamed of?" the brilliant essayist asks. We are all hopping in our seats to share our regrets, our secrets. Two hundred writers overflow the lecture hall. We've dragged chairs in from an adjacent room, crammed ourselves into windowsills, and lined up leaning against the cabinets along the back wall. She moves on to great first lines and titles. Stunning ideas burst forth: pithy headlines and bold openings. She shows us some of hers. Inspiring! We are excited and engaged, snapping pictures of her slides. We're here to learn from a teacher who's written a bunch of essays we all love, a writer we all admire. She has published essays in all the magazines and journals we want to publish our essays in. She is famous and talented, funny, clever, and bright.

I teach writing too. I'm compelled to teach though I struggle to master the skills. It may be true, what they say about teachers: that those who can, do; and those who can't, teach. I know which one I am, but the mean-spirited cliché doesn't hurt my feelings. On the contrary, I've come to believe in the value of struggling to do what I teach.

Ask anybody in my family, and they'll tell you that my Nana Rose, our olive-skinned, gray-haired, not five-feet-tall Sicilian great-grandmother who immigrated to the US as a teenager, was the best cook in the world. She made pasta and bread from scratch and spent all her time in the kitchen.

As a child, I assisted my aging Nana, holding up long sheets of pasta to crank through the machine or stirring a sauce pot. I remember windows steaming up from the gently gurgling sauce, on a burner since sunrise, and how everything smelled of onions and sausage. I remember flour and tomato smeared all over my front, my hands, my arms. Cooking with Nana was a sensual experience, an inspiration I still carry with me in the kitchen.

My mother was a lousy cook but another sort of teacher: first grade. She wanted the family recipes down on paper. She had an index card and a pencil, and she intended to use them. She required details, instructions. "Wait, how much sausage do you put in the *pannuzzi?*" Mom would ask, scribbling over our shoulders while we rolled handfuls of dough around spoons full of meat.

"Put how much-a you like," Nana yelled at her, almost knocking the pencil from her hands with a wooden spoon.

How much-a you like could not be more specific, yet it's also subjective, not measurable, unknowable. Nana didn't cook in a way you could write down. She cooked by taste and feel. Cooking with her thrilled me; having learned to cook from her feels magical. One day it mystified me, and years later, my hands just knew the texture of risen bread; my teeth, the bite of perfect, *al dente* pasta. I don't remember Nana explaining these things. She wasn't that kind of teacher.

The celebrated essayist opens it up for questions, and I shake myself out of my hot-ideas-brainstorm frenzy long enough to connect to my own essay writing challenges. Do I have a question?

Yes! I do have a question! Structure! It drives me crazy in my essays. How do I tell a personal story and weave it in with some enlightenment? Is it weaving or braiding or twisting? Do you write down each story and then sketch out your big idea separately? Then arrange them? Or do you write the whole essay from beginning to end? When my own writing students ask questions like this, I drag out my plot structure charts, or we dissect and study the structures of another story or essay they love.

"Can you talk about structure?" I ask, notepad and pen poised. I can't wait to see her structure slide!

I became a teacher before I started teaching writing, back when I was a sex worker, escorting and dancing nude. I picked up an unusual gig teaching medical students how to give pelvic exams, a unique job for activists and sex workers—perfect for me. I brought skills like sexual boldness, fierce stage presence, confident physical boundaries, and emotional generosity.

Those show-off skills landed the job, but to keep it, I had to become a different kind of teacher: one that instructs. I spent the next fifteen years showing three students at a time my genitals and guiding them through exam steps and speculum wielding.

This gig eventually took over all my sex-work time and turned me into a full-time teacher. Sensitive exam instruction is intimate and detailed. It is not easy to identify an ovary on the first try. It can be scary to open a speculum inside a vagina. You have to really use your imagination to palpate the uterus with two hands. And also, the teacher is wearing no pants.

This kind of teaching corrects gently, closely, with exactness. It requires something more than showing oneself as example, nudging a talent, encouraging instincts, or telling students to feel their way. Step-by-step instructions never read, "put how much-a you like."

"Promise to be your most fumbly, spongey student self," I told my students. "I will tell you what to do. This is not about achievement; it's about practice." Teaching sex causes giggling, squirming, and discomfort, but in the safe confines of step-by-step instruction, students cope with the struggle to learn by asking questions.

"Do piercings hurt?"

"Is this a normal amount of hair?"

"Can I look at the cervix again?"

Teaching by example is popular. Learners want to admire our teachers, to believe they are better than we are at this thing they are teaching us. We want to learn to write a novel from a bestselling novelist, to learn to swim from an Olympic champion, but setting an inspiring example is not the only way to teach. As students, we might think we want encouragement more than correction. Admirable, enviable teachers pack classrooms, put butts in seats.

Inspired by my medical students, I developed a female pleasure anatomy class for men at my local feminist sex-toy store. The name of the class, *Girl-Girl Tricks for Men*, implied girl-on-girl action with a side of education, but my curriculum offered steps and tips. I did not entertain by showing off secrets from the lesbian bed. Instead, my workshop featured an anatomically correct vulva puppet and several diagrams. I offered maps, exercises. We talked about how to identify and gently approach the clitoris, labia, urethral opening, and peri-urethral gland. We discussed things like variation in touch, consent, and the tactile limitations of a penis compared to a hand. I did not tell these students to feel their way. I did not tell them to *put how much-a you like*.

I used to think that sex work and then sex ed attracted me because I was good at sex, but I think instead that I came to sex education, sex work, and, before that, even my lesbian identity because mashing genitals and groping in the dark were not getting me the sexual satisfaction I needed.

Feeling broken drove me to pick up the pieces. Struggling, I started asking questions. And that humbled me, made me examine the assumptions, the defaults, and the heteronormative paradigm itself. It made me examine my own underbelly. My patience increased for others while they explored theirs. Examining the broken pieces made it possible to teach others about sex.

I must remember this when I feel like an impostor among my more well-established writing-teacher colleagues. The teacher cliché creates a double bind for us, especially for a teacher like me, who backed into teaching writing before launching my writing career. I don't feel I have permission to teach this because I have no experience or success at it, and I'm teaching it because I'm not yet successful enough to earn my living doing it. This double bind is my answer to the essayist's brilliant, challenging question: What am I ashamed of? I am ashamed—sometimes—of being a writing teacher without having achieved the identity of writer.

The workshop leader responds to my structure inquiry with a blank look. I've asked a stupid question. "It's just, 'This happened,' and then, 'this happened,' and then, 'this happened,'" she tells me, as if it's obvious.

She is my Nana, but she has a laser pointer instead of a wooden spoon. She doesn't know how she does it. She just does it in an order that feels right to her. There's something about mechanics, the structure of a gorgeous, complex, prize-winning essay, that just makes sense to her, that she just gets. This and then this. How much-a you like.

I drop my pen, lest she knock it from my hand with her laser pointer. I don't get it, I think to myself, baffled by her answer. I will go home from this workshop and outline one of her essays, maybe two, to try to figure out what she means.

"I don't get how you can cook like that," Mom would say, baffled by Nana's sure and swift hands.

Maybe the natural talents just get it. They feel their way. Put how much you like. It's just this and this and this. That's why I like Maya Angelou's revision: "When you learn, teach. When you get, give." She attributes the idea to her grandmother, and it commands both kinds of teachers.

The getters should give. The learners should teach. To do is to give, to lead by example. If you get it—whether you naturally understand it or legitimately inherited the talent—do it. Give us your beautiful example. Show us, so we can watch. Inspire us. Make it look easy, even. The other teachers—the ones who must learn it through struggle—will work with labor, repetition, patience, instruction. Put this finger here. Hold the speculum like this.

I leave the workshop uninspired, not needing any more ideas for essays. I have a one-hundred-page document full of snappy opening lines already on my laptop. I need instruction. My essays and stories do not fall out of me in an easy, "this happened," then, "this happened," manner. I need to grapple with how to uncover the richest veins of content, how to balance personal stories with research, when to expand, and where to contract.

But maybe I'm looking for another kind of inspiration. I want to write essays like her, sure. But I want to fill a classroom like she does, too, or maybe I just want the permission she has to teach, the validation of my credentials to instruct in spite of my struggle to learn and achieve.

Last year, a dear friend and writing buddy of mine died. Dave had come to me to be his writing teacher a few years prior, but like all my favorite clients, he had become my teacher as well. When I attended his memorial, everyone who spoke about him mentioned this characteristic, his ability to quickly ascend from acolyte to teacher in their relationships—as a Buddhist, as a friend, as a lover—just as he had with me as a writer and editor.

When I visited him at home a few days before he died, he was so happy. He told me he'd always wanted to host a series of visits like ours with people from all the circles of his life. He told me he couldn't wait for me to see the memorial he was planning for himself. "Do you want to see my shroud?" he asked me with all the gusto of a bride-to-be offering a peek at her wedding dress.

Everyone who attended his memorial had these laughable stories about things he'd said to them in his final days too. Our laughter gave way to sincere expressions that we all wanted to die just the way Dave did. He, as we all do, must have entered his death phase an acolyte, but he left the earth as our teacher. "Here you go, my friends. Here's how to do death."

And that's what it is to be a teacher, I think. Nobody goes into death with experience or knowing how to do it. Enter as a humble student. Be courageous enough to lead by example. Share your best learning with generosity, specificity, and sincere curiosity. Coordinate visits with friends in your last days. Choose a shroud you really love.

WHAT WE SHARE

Ashley Trebisacci

The first time a person comes out to me, I'm a sophomore in college. I'm enrolled in an Introduction to Gender Studies class, and it is at once helping me put the pieces of my life together and absolutely blowing my mind.

Professor Gibbons (who says we should call her Josie, but this is still hard for us) is sitting at her usual spot in our discussion circle, looking visibly on-edge. Today, we are learning about feminist pedagogy; for homework, we've read a selection from bell hooks's *Teaching to Transgress*. As a lover of school, and of learning, I'm particularly moved by this piece. The proof is in my emphatic marginalia, where exclamation points and hearts are scribbled around heavily underlined passages. Josie tells us bell hooks writes that in order to create a culture of trust in the classroom, you must be honest with your students. If you expect your students to share their lives with you, you must be willing to share your life with them. At this point, she wrings her hands, takes a breath, and looks around at us before saying: "And so, in keeping with that, I want to tell you all . . . that I'm gay."

It's like the air has been sucked out of the room. I realize then that I've never met a real-life lesbian, and furthermore, that I've never considered that one could be teaching at a Catholic college. As I glance around the room, it becomes clear that we are all shocked, and a little shaken by the fact that our generally so composed professor seems anxious about this admission. The silence feels full of something, though—a kind of awe, a quiet reverence. We recognize that we have been given a gift, but, as we're only a few weeks into our Gender Studies education, we don't yet know how to respond to it.

A year later, when I tell Josie that I think I'm a lesbian, she will congratulate me. I'll find this hilarious and so, so weird. Who congratulates someone on being gay?

Three years after that, when one of my students comes out to me, I will congratulate him. It will come out naturally, as if it was my own idea to say it.

***

In the spring of our junior year, my friend Meg develops an absurd theory that Josie's partner also works at the College, that she is an English professor named Nora.

At this time, I am studying abroad in England and am having some unexpected revelations with regard to my own relationships. Mainly, I'm finally coming to terms with the idea that a former female friend of mine had, in fact, been more than a friend. Though we never acknowledged it aloud, and though our friendship imploded shortly before I left for England, I am now starting to make sense of the hand-holding, beginning to equate the longing I felt with what I know to be true about desire.

Meg is also having some ambiguous-female-friendship drama, so we've been communicating even more than usual, wading through our confusion together despite being on opposite sides of the Atlantic. On this occasion, she Skypes me from her dorm room, where she is hanging out with our friend, Caroline. They are both taking a class with the professor Meg suspects to be Josie's partner. The class is, ironically (or perhaps not ironically), centered on the idea of "passing." Meg makes one last-ditch attempt to convince us her theory is plausible:

"Haven't you ever noticed their pedagogies are eerily similar?" (Meg, it should be noted, is an Education major, and is highly attuned to the ways in which teachers teach.) "They both ask us to call them by their first names. They both have their classes sit in a circle . . ." The list of similarities goes on, until Caroline interjects: "They both have ten fingers and ten toes!"

We dissolve into giggles, but Meg is not easily deterred. "Also, I might have done some research. They both went to the University of Chicago, where they presented at some conferences together." Caroline and I admit this part is compelling, applaud Meg on her commitment to solving what feels to us like a pretty intriguing mystery, but remain unconvinced. We also remind her that there is virtually no way to get proof of this without revealing that we've creepily pried into our professors' personal lives.

Months pass, and while the list of reasons continues to grow, we haven't been able to put together the pieces. When I return to campus the following fall, I visit Josie in her office, and I swear I see a picture of Nora—a tiny dot of a person standing on a craggy coastline—tacked to the bulletin board behind her desk. I can't find the nerve to lean in a little further and confirm I am right, though, and can't summon the words to actually ask her about it.

Looking back, I'm inclined to believe that Meg and I actually enjoyed being in suspense, that we needed a reason to fixate our questions about queer relationships on something (or someone) outside of ourselves. That we relished being able to talk about same-sex partnerships all the time without having to acknowledge what they might mean to us. That we loved imagining the possibility of two women we admired being in love with each other.

Later that semester, we'll find out that Nora is pregnant. Meg will be meeting with a different English professor one afternoon, who will casually remark that Josie and Nora are having twins. My phone will blow up with texts from Meg, sent in all capitals.

***

In December of my senior year, I kiss a friend in a parking garage. It's my first girl kiss, and it's all very romantic. I am beside myself—wholly overcome by a rush of joy and wanting—and need to tell Josie immediately. Unfortunately, it's Sunday.

On Monday morning, I'm in her office as soon as possible, my limbs still humming from the rush of adrenaline. "Hi! Guess what? I kissed a girl. And I liked it." (Katy Perry is very popular right now, and I am delighted to keep making this reference.)

Besides the slight eyebrow raise, she seems unfazed. She replies with a sincere: "I'm happy for you."

I'm going to need a bit more than that from her. This is one of the most significant moments of my young life—and certainly the most significant of my newly-embarked-upon lady-loving life. "I just . . . I can't stop smiling. And I can't get any work done. Is it always like this? What am I supposed to do now?"

That gets me a smirk, and a non-answer: "There's no right way to do this."

Typical. I am more than a little displeased with this standard brand of Josie advice. Meg and I often complain to each other about how evasive she can be, how she has a maddening habit of flipping your questions back on you and forcing you to sit in your uncertainty rather than helping you figure out an answer. Once, I tried to tell her how much this drove me crazy, and she chalked it up to her not being particularly nurturing. I know she is, deep down, which is why I continue to come to her with my every life crisis, but she's definitely not living up to her potential today. With an eye-roll and a resigned "fiiiiine," I turn to head out the door. Before I'm fully in the hall, she calls out: "Oh, and Ashley? Write your paper."

Two years later, I'll participate in a panel presentation with other openly LGBTQ faculty and staff at the college where I work. One of the students in the audience will ask me to share the best piece of advice I've ever received on the topic of being out and queer. I'll hesitate, smile, and tell them: "There's no right way to do this."

***

In the weeks after graduation, Josie hires me as her research assistant. We meet to discuss the logistics of our arrangement at Seven Stars, a hip bakery/coffee shop in her city, which is about forty-five minutes away from my parents' house. I feel so adult going to my first real meeting over coffee, and so thrilled that Josie likes me enough to keep me around.

The meeting itself isn't all that notable, except for the feeling I get halfway through. The one that tells me we've shifted a little, have both settled into a more relaxed friendliness even though this is, technically speaking, still a professional relationship.

By this time, the girl I kissed in the parking garage has become my girlfriend. The next time we visit the city, I'll take her to Seven Stars. We'll eat lemon cakes and drink tea and soak up the intellectual hipster vibes and praise Josie for her excellent taste. Eventually, we'll spend hours there, reading and writing and talking and watching a steady stream of teenage ballerinas come and go from the dancing school across the street.

Much later, after we move seven hundred miles away, we'll find a recipe for the lemon cakes in a back issue of the city's newspaper and try to recreate them in our kitchen. I'll marvel at the fact that Josie seemed to lead me to this, too.

***

When the fall comes around again, my job as Josie's research assistant expands to include the following roles: house sitter, cat sitter, and babysitter for the twins, who are now almost nine months old. The more titles I gain, the less I am able to explain what Josie and I are to each other. It's an ambiguity I am entirely comfortable with, one that I embrace wholeheartedly.

In her home, things are different, and the same. She is always herself, but I feel different each time I visit. Like I am getting closer to something—a kind of comfort, a kind of ease. Like I am becoming part of the family. I learn which plants to water, and how much. I learn how to convince her cat to take his pills. I learn which route is the best for the boys' afternoon walk. I learn how to make them laugh by spinning them round and round.

Before long, I'll come to feel Josie's home is a second home, a place where I feel most like myself. When I'm alone there, I relish the chance to continue my lesbian education. I read Nora's copy of *Passing*. I take all of Josie's Indigo Girls CDs and upload them to my iTunes. I find every framed picture of Josie and Nora that I can and gush over their cuteness.

Sometimes, my babysitting skills are enlisted even when moms are both home, when they are trying to write or grade papers. Sometimes, this turns into me staying for dinner. On these days I am an even more diligent observer, though I don't always realize that I am taking copious mental notes. I pay attention to who grills the meat and who makes the salad. I pay attention to how they parent, how they complement each other, how their love can be contained in a glance or a gesture.

Later, after my girlfriend and I have been living together for a few months, I'll notice who washes the dishes and who dries them, who leaves notes on the fridge and who answers them, how we seem to fit together just as naturally as they did.

***

In graduate school, I'll find another wonderful lady-loving professor/mentor/role model/friend. (This will not be a complete coincidence, for I know I still have things to learn.)

She will mean all that Josie meant to me, and maybe more. At the end of the year, as we start to transition into something beyond the teacher-student bond, I'll ask her the things I was too shy to ask Josie: "When did you know you were gay?" "How did you meet your wife?" She will give me all of her answers, and then some.

In the time in-between, I will have publicly declared my sexuality countless times: to my family, to my friends, to my coworkers, to my students. I'll have written my graduate thesis on the effect of study abroad on my lesbian identity development. I'll have served as an LGBTQ Resource Center Coordinator. I'll have joked that I have managed to make a career out of coming out.

Some days, I will feel like I never learned anything at all. I will be convinced there was a right way to do this, and that I messed it up. I will wring my hands with anxiety. I will give my students non-answers. But on other days, I will manage to do the best thing that Josie taught me: to share my life with someone, and, in doing so, open a world.

PROTECT YOUR FEMME

Shivani Davé

i paint my sharp nails gold this winter to remind me of the sun and hard earned self-worth. fabric stretched tight across my chest, i strut past the wax parlor. my belly full, legs unruly. i weave in and out of numb fingers fumbling for touch, balancing their desire and mine with a commitment to self.

protect your femme. they'll tell you to rip out your hair and tame your glare. claim the contours of your body are grips to help them climb. return you docile and delicate.

i trade the orders to self mutilate for self poked tattoos, scars of anxiety turned to art and ask her to teach me how to fight. never held fists to shield my face, only offer my wrists in embrace. so when she swings, i see outstretched arms and barrel into her waist.

protect your femme, they'll tell you to tread water in the trauma and ride unconditional forgiveness to the crest. to forgo the high tides of healing and submit to appeasing.

but when she pulls up to the curb and i strap into the
passenger seat, i raise my chin, part my lips and beckon her in. tender and tough my femme gives me a place to rest, a steady fire lapping up their inconsistencies.

i pull the breaks, she swerves a patiently waits.
my femme is unwavering, head held high, hips cocked to the side, living this warm in the dead of cold warrior.

AWAY GAME

Jillian Etheridge

The high school band was loading onto the bus in their black pants, suspenders pulled over red shirts that read "Mandel High School Band" with an iron-on of a black-and-white circus tent. Miss Myers sat in the driver's seat reading a glossy teen magazine. She pulled her dirty blonde hair back into a baseball cap. Tonight was football. Miss Myers was driving the band to the game about an hour away in Laurence, just outside of Oak, Mississippi. She was elbow-deep in an article about Jordan, a young black boy the police had shot during a birthday party, when the assistant band director stepped onto the bus. He had shaved his beard into a goatee because the band director said goatees were more professional. He was wearing a wind suit with "Mandel High School Band" printed across the back and held a clipboard under his right arm. He leaned into her seat so the kids could pass, left arm slung over her seatback.

"Almost loaded up, Myers. What you got there? A magazine?"

"Yeah, just finding some articles for analysis." She held up the magazine, showing him the cover. "We're studying different ways we define heroes. The ways we redefine heroes for a cause, in this case."

"Out of a female magazine?" He rubbed his goatee in his left hand's fingers, elbow jutting into her seatback. "You think the kids are going to be into that crap?"

Miss Myers flipped through the magazine, holding her finger on her place. She closed the magazine and checked the spine, ducking her head under it. "I just don't see a vagina on it, Porter."

"Good god, Myers. What?"

"Magazine doesn't have a vagina." She smiled at him, the type of lady-smile to let the man know it was a joke.

He grumbled and walked down the aisle with his clipboard, checking names off the roster. Band members were reaching across seats for gum, for snacks, for skin, popping each other's suspenders, ruffling each other's hair and feathers. Miss Myers went back to her magazine.

Going south down old highway 290, the afternoon light was strobing through the trees. Miss Myers hated it. Made her feel disoriented. She had moved to Mandel the summer before school started. This was her first year driving a school bus, first time driving the band to an away football game. She thought it would be a nice extra income and had fond memories of riding a bumpy school bus home, not two hours north of Mandel, near the capital. Her bus driver was ruthless, sped over speed bumps and small animals, jumped curbs. Once, a kid bounced so high his head hit the roof, and he nearly bit his tongue clean off. A well-endowed girl ripped her top off to stop his bleeding mouth. The bus driver pulled over to assess the situation. As he walked to the back of the bus, he ripped off his sunglasses.

"Rose, what—why is your shirt off?" the bus driver had asked, leering obviously at her lacy bra.

The kids were still rowdy, twenty years later; the road wound around creeks and farmland; the engine stuttered. It was familiar, yet new, because she was no longer in the middle aisle, but in the front, driving. She was no longer in the suburbs, but in the sticks.

The signs of different little stick towns amused her. Summerland. Soso. Gitano. Lebanon. Jesus, Mississippi. Each town a new maze of grindy roads she would never go down, stores she would never venture into, donut and breakfast places where men with pomade hair ate their breakfasts once their wives died.

Mandel felt safe. Everyone was welcoming. One of her students, a light-skinned boy, wore his uniform with vibrancy and lip gloss, sometimes tied a scarf around his neck. A girl of hers wore Boy Attire, preferred Rob instead of Roberta. When Miss Myers had her interview, the principal and lead teacher notified her of these things.

"We have a very diverse student body," the principal had said while the lead teacher chuckled into her right shoulder.

"Yes," the lead teacher had said. "We have an over seventy-five percent black student body, and many students who are exploring their gender, if you will."

"Great," Miss Myers had replied. She understood why they had told her. She was an average white woman with an extreme type A personality, ever-worried about turning in lesson plans and paperwork, getting her grades in within a day of the assignment. Miss Myers had nothing outside of the school, the students thought. She and Gwen were always at school events. She cheered for the golf team, the speech and debate team. She and Gwen came to homecoming to chaperone.

One day in class, a student asked her, "How long have you and Gwen been friends?"

Miss Myers thought for only a second before replying, "We were college roommates."

"Is she married?"

"Not yet." Miss Myers, however, was dreaming of the day she would ask Gwen to marry her, the ring ever-present in her purse.

A clearing came, bringing sunlight to the bus route. A barn overrun with vines collapsed to the west, shadow cast in front. Miss Myers thought she saw someone move but focused back on the road. The skinny shadow-dog snooped around in the barn for scraps that no one left because no one was there to leave any scraps. A copperhead rested in the leaves.

The bus swerved around a long curve on the outskirts of Oak. There was a narrow abandoned two-story building, much longer than it was wide. And in the middle of nowhere, Miss Myers knew where she was. The feeling of knowing in the midst of ignorance. The smell of leather, like the smell of tires, came to her. She remembered being in that building, not able to reach the tops of the racks filled with denim jackets. Rows of jeans and cowboy boots, saddles hanging on the wall. Kenny Rogers faintly singing in the background. A smell she didn't want to leave. Leather and denim, face pressed against the rough smoothness of the jean jacket. It was only a flash, a happy memory that she couldn't quite grasp. She'd definitely been in that building, once upon a time, when it was a store for cowboys. Smelling of leather.

A stop sign disrupted her thoughts. She took a deep breath while the band kids stood in the back, Mr. Porter screaming at them to sit as the bus came to an abrupt halt. One kid gasped as his stomach landed on the back of the seat in front of him, his head crashing into a girl with braces. The girl punched him on the top of the head. The boy yelled his innocence as girls stood from the seats, pointing and blowing up. The boy was not big enough to take on angry teenage girls. Not nearly big enough. Miss Myers caught a glimpse in the mirror as Mr. Porter stepped between them and others stood behind the boy. Mr. Porter pulled his clipboard out from under his arm to write a note as the girls shook their heads. They sat down, and the girl with braces started crying between her clenched teeth. The boy, confused and pissed that his accident kept escalating, continued yelling at the girls as the girl with braces sobbed ugly tears.

The bus rolled on.

Once they arrived at Lawrence High School, a shitty little school, Mr. Porter suggested that Miss Myers stick to the main highway.

"I know it's a little longer of a drive, but that road there. You're going to see a lot of deer. I'm just looking out for you." He grabbed onto her shoulder, squeezing just before he released her.

Miss Myers agreed; she knew the main highway better than the route they'd taken. The highway would add twenty minutes to their trip, but the smell of leather. She couldn't risk getting distracted again. She drove the highway often to Oak to see Gwen.

At the concession stand, little ladies rushed around in bright green shirts, LHS PTO emblazoned across their chests. The couple in front of Miss Myers couldn't have been more than freshmen: the girl, leaning back on the railing and laughing; the boy, flipping his hair and tucking it behind his ear. The girl looked to the ground, blushed. The boy looked up. It was their turn. The boy ordered a bunch of candy for the girl and felt in his pockets for his wallet.

Once Miss Myers had her nachos and Coke she walked towards the bleachers. Small children were running on either side for no particular reason. She got a spot just as the "Star-Spangled Banner" began. She placed her nachos on the gritty bleacher and put her hand over her heart. A man beside her cleared his throat and looked at her hat. She took her hat off, placed it over her heart as well. She wondered how her hair looked in the bright lights.

Cheerleaders in white and green marched onto the field with a bunch of green balloons. A woman came on the PA system.

"We would like to take a moment of silence to remember Kylie Emmerson, a young girl whose life was taken all too soon in an automobile accident earlier this week. Kylie passed away this morning." A moment went by. "And now, we will release balloons to heaven for her." The cheerleaders let go of their balloons. The balloons rose just out of the cheerleaders' reach when the PA voice cheered, "Now let's play some football!" The bleachers vibrated with the stomping of feet.

Miss Myers thought back to the night her high school PA system announced the death of a student. No one had known before the announcement. She had been standing beside her older brother.

"It is a sad night tonight at Reeves High. Mitch Roberts was in an accident earlier today, so we would like to take a moment of silence." That was all she remembered hearing before watching her brother's face crunch into itself and turn to her. She absorbed his tears into her T-shirt, not really knowing what to say or do, so she just stood there and let others grab her as well, absorbing all their sadness into herself. She didn't know Mitch as anyone except a guy who occasionally came over to work on cars with her brother, but he had spent several nights in the room next to hers, playing video games.

The man beside Miss Myers leaned in. "How you doing?"

Miss Myers smiled and chewed, signaling with her finger that she was chewing, before replying. "I'm good, real good. How are you, Mr. Evans?"

"Oh, call me Frank. I'm doing fine, fine. Such a nice night. We're about to crush these guys. Sammie has been pumped all week for this game." He took a swig of his Coke. After he swallowed, he asked, "How is Sammie doing anyway? He isn't giving you too much trouble is he?"

Miss Myers wondered if she could catalogue this as a parent-teacher conference. "No, not really. I mean, he seems to be a little more focused on his phone and socializing some days, but no more than anyone else."

"Oh, he's being bad in class?" Frank rubbed the tops of his thighs.

"No, not that. I just mean that his grades would be better off if he focused. Same as any of my students, really. I let them do things on their phones sometimes, but some days, I think, you know, maybe they shouldn't rely so much on that." Miss Myers laughed a wispy little laugh.

Frank took a breath and let it out of his mouth forcefully. "How bad is his grade now? Is he failing?"

"No, he is not failing."

"Well," Frank cocked his head, chin jabbed towards her. "What's the grade? What's the damage? Because he can get better. I can make sure of that."

"I don't know off the top of my head." She looked at her chips, which were getting soggy under the weight of the extra cheese. "You know, you can check on his grades online at any time."

"Can you show me?" Frank scooted closer. "Can you get into your gradebook from my phone?"

"You know, Sammie is doing fine in class. I was just saying he's a teenage boy, and like most of the other students, he can improve. All students can improve."

"So he has an A?"

Miss Myers shrugged. "I don't exactly know his grade off the top of my head."

Frank laughed under his breath as he put his phone back in his pocket. "I'm sorry. It's been a hectic year for Sammie. He's just not the same since his mom and I divorced." He took another swig of his Coke and glanced at her. "You're a pretty lady. Anyone taking you out?"

"Sorry, I have to use the ladies' room."

"I'll keep your seat warm."

"Thanks," she said as she got up and shuffled down the bleachers to freedom. The ladies' room was not quite the respite she wanted. She entered the available stall and saw a thick layer of wet, yellowed toilet paper covering the seat. She looked at the other stalls and could see other women squatting over the toilets. The doors barely grazed her shoulders. She joined the squatting women, hovered over the piss-soaked, toilet paper–coated toilet. When she was finished, she reached into the dispenser, but there was no more toilet paper. It was all on the seat inches under her.

"Could someone hand me some toilet paper?" she asked.

A girl beside her with bright red fingernails shoved toilet paper under the stall wall, a curtain of it grazing the floor.

"Thanks."

"No problem, Miss Myers."

At halftime, Miss Myers found herself watching the Lawrence High band do a melody of Michael Jackson songs, girls twirling red flags. One of her students nudged her.

"Look behind you."

Miss Myers turned around. There was Gwen. Gwen smiled, holding her palms forward, and Miss Myers felt her face flush. Miss Myers wondered if half the students knew who Michael Jackson was as the drum major grabbed his crotch and the entire band yelled at the end of the show.

The football game started back up as Gwen and Miss Myers walked back and forth in front of the visitors' bleachers.

"How's the game been so far?"

"I don't even want to think about it. I was planning on calling you later and telling you all about it. The food is awful. I don't understand the game. Everyone knows me." They leaned against the chain-link fence.

"Everyone knows you everywhere we ever go, Liz. We could be in Cincinnati, and I'm sure you could run into someone you knew in undergrad."

"Maybe. I think John from my study group lives there now. Married to some girl from New Jersey. Anyway, I had this weird feeling earlier. I found a place I had seen before."

"We've been to Lawrence before."

"No, as a child. I had been there, at this country Western store. It's abandoned now." The Mandel High School football team scored again. The fight song started playing. "I feel like I'm always being watched. I can't enjoy a margarita at a restaurant without a student coming to talk to me."

Gwen laughed. "I don't have that problem. My coworkers, however, sometimes they'll be at the bar and want to talk when I'm out with friends."

"It's stupid." Miss Myers looked at the players running around, the students happy. She thought about the ring in her purse, her purse on the bus, the bus locked up. She wondered if a high school football game was a good time to propose. If it would change anything. If it would free her. Or. She looked at Gwen. "Just self-conscious, I guess."

Soon, the game ended. The students needed a ride back to Mandel, and Gwen had to go home and clean her litter boxes. The ring waited patiently.

On the main highway, Miss Myers enjoyed the silence of the students. Many were falling asleep after the long night of revelry. The football team had slaughtered, winning by a landslide in the final quarter. In the mirror, she saw some students with phones lighting up their faces. She wished she could text Gwen, let her know she was glad she had come to the game, but she kept her eyes on the road as other cars swerved in and out of lanes.

Mr. Porter sat behind her on his phone. He leaned forward.

"I saw your friend came." He smacked his lips. "Are you two together?"

A deer leaped into the road and cast itself against the front of the bus with a snap. It flew through the air, a brief look of disdain on his face, and landed with his antlers in the back window of a dark-colored car.

"Holy fuck, holy fuck, holy fuck," Mr. Porter started as Miss Myers glided the bus to the side of the road.

Students were awake, standing and looking out of all the windows. The girl with braces had a slide of drool on her cheek as she stared out of the front glass. The car pulled over, antler through the back window, body dragging across the asphalt. Miss Myers's hands were white against the wheel.

"Keep calm," she heard her teacher-voice saying as she got up and walked off the bus. Other cars were pulling over, the other buses too. The convoy back to Mandel pulled over. Miss Myers wished they would go on. Traffic was slowing down behind them. The people in the car got out, a young couple. Miss Myers barely saw the man in his tracksuit coming towards her.

"Are you okay? Is everyone okay?" He asked her.

"Yes, we're okay. Are you okay?"

The man looked at the dying deer moaning on the back of their car. "He isn't. I think he's a goner."

Other bus drivers were gathering. What was the procedure?

Mr. Porter came down to talk to the couple. Miss Myers went back into the bus and pulled out a pack of cigarettes. As she walked by the other bus drivers, she heard them murmur, but she didn't let that stop her from lighting up. She stopped in front of the deer-stabbed car. She figured the students could still see her. As she inhaled, she looked across the wide highway and saw something she had never seen on this road she drove weekly: a huge estate on a lake. Another moment like with the leather store, but the opposite. A tangible epiphany of five-story housing, surrounded by smaller bungalows. She discovered a lake in the middle of it all, new and reflecting the full moon and the small orange streetlights in perfect stillness. An iron fence surrounded the whole ordeal.

Inside, a few of the elderly residents of the nursing home watched the blue lights racing towards the buses as they thought about the chances they never took.

LOCAL KNOWLEDGE

Jay Whittaker

East Lothian oaks, transplanted
from French estates,
conceal a cache of truffles
for those who know where to look.

As for Hailes castle,
Bothwell's birthplace,
more residence than fortress,
marital problems quoth an info-board—

you told me
there was a porn shoot here
hard to imagine anything
but goosebumps.

NOTHING RATTLES THE DJ

Robin Reagler

On the dance floor we breathe in sync as music files into our lungs the pulse commandeering our body the all the one with all the other ones here we are heat we are flashing free of gender, cages, terms we are a game of feels we are blindness split into rhythm, neon dissected by beats, we are more than electric we are young, free, motherless, sweet as hell, grieving, sweltering just-born bodies queering validation, donning invisible haloes underneath planetary lights and music is the rope harness holding us onto the face of the sheer cliff

    language is the drug kissing is the muscularity hips hold the rhyme high above us is the DJ wearing the matador hat and smiling for the love and beauty of the bulls we mouth non-messages to one another there's nothing to say pleasure is a poem you are tulips on a winter morning we are in love with you and you and you (us loving the all of us) and the cylinder of sound swells into sun, blaze, brain beeping, constellations of lucky stars and until you say when it will never end never end never ever end

SLACK

Mo Fowler

It was a beach where bad things happen. That was clear from the first time R went. The entire scene was a deep green settling in the back of your throat, the kind of bad that heals you like whiskey for a sore throat. Fifteen miles from school, it was where she and K waited out all of their hangovers, half-asleep on the wooden benches with the flannel blankets R kept in her trunk. The fog was rising as afternoon approached. It rested on her shoulders and made R grip tighter to the mittens bundled in the crumb-filled pockets of her jacket. She leaned against the door of the car, her thumbs pressed down so hard that she could feel her nails digging through the cotton and into her hands. They'd be leaving soon. K had promised her that before running back down to the water, where she'd left the car keys tucked against the bench they'd spent the morning on. R made a slow circle with her body, looking across the parking lot filled with cars with sand stains up to their waists and windshields wiped barely clean enough to make it back to the highway.

She started back down the stairs descending the side of the cliff, hoping that walking would stretch the goosebumps out of her skin. It was their second or third time going, and she wasn't used to the wind yet. Catching K in her peripherals, she kept her face straight ahead, not wanting her to know that she'd seen her. She watched K notice her, watched her wipe the palms of her hands on the back of her jeans. K pushed the hair off her forehead and turned back towards the water. *Watch me watch you.*

R knows what they look like as they walk in, legs bared, jeans high on their waists and more ripped than together. It is the first party K has invited her to. They sit in R's car in the parking lot outside the club eating pizza-flavored Pringles out of the can. K licks sunset dust off her palm and tucks what's left of the tube into her blue leather backpack. They'd spent the afternoon on the rug of her bedroom, both half-asleep and passing notes in a composition book K kept under her bed for their secrets. The book was thick with ticket stubs and empty condom wrappers. The invite had come almost on accident, because R happened to still be laying there when K got the address. And R had a car, and agreed to stay sober, and had no other plans to attend to.

K zips her backpack and sits back up, leaning over to test a lipstick on R's shoulder—"Thank god you never tan." R shifts the strap of her tank top to make sure it won't rub against the runaway plum line of makeup that now snakes nearly to her collarbone. They smear thick gold glitter mixed with glue across the fronts of their legs, the paste sticking to hairs and scabs and moving like batter across the canvas of their limbs. The ripped strings of the jeans get caught in the mixture, sticking to their knees as they step into the party. The music shakes the doorjamb as R's hand brushes past it and her heart beats sick and small.

"I wish we were worth this place," K says, her fingers on the inside of R's elbow as they push past the initial crush of the crowds at the door. It is part of K's game where she reminds them they are horrible, part of the game where she points out when the skin of R's stomach hangs over the edge of her pants, when R's makeup is not enough or too much or too much like hers—"God, stop trying to steal my soul."

K squeezes R's hand, kisses her cheek, takes a shot of tequila and walks into the party. She is always moving forward, always keeping R behind her.

It was a beach where bad things happen. R slid back out of the boots she hadn't bothered to tie, their bottoms crusted with damp mud from the parking lot. It was four in the morning, or maybe closer to five now, and weeks since they'd started coming here.

She'd been sleeping in the car for nearly an hour. She left the boots at the edge of the concrete, slid a sock into each one, and pressed her toes into the cool grains of sand. K stood halfway between her and the water, the wind throwing her green jacket against her skin in pulses and her hair high into the air where it hung obsidian against the clouds.

R's jeans were damp to nearly the knee from jumping waves. It had seemed like a good idea a couple hours ago, but now the wet fabric grew leaden with sand as she walked.

K raised her eyes from the rocks to the water when R walked up. She smiled with the side of her mouth R could see. *I love you even when it's scary*. R's heart rate slowed, going from a live thing beating at her temples to a small fur in the back of her throat, warm with knowing she was still necessary, even if only as a body for K to bounce off of. R tried to keep herself from feeling better being around her, but just because.

K was the one person in her life saying that she loved her. And then, *God, stop being so annoying*, and then, *I just feel really hurt when you hang out with them instead of me*, and then no more them and then no more R.

The next week she wasn't invited. It kept her up all night and Sunday morning R rolled over to check her phone. Felt bored seeing that none of the texts were from K. Her stomach felt tight and cold at the lack. She stared at the wall for twenty minutes and then replied to her cousin's string of texts from the night before, *just because i can see that she isn't treating me well doesn't mean i'm at the point of realizing that i deserve to be treated well*.

You can't love someone just because they are almost as good at hating you as you are.

You're worth more than waiting for her.

An hour later, the text came. R jumped. On the beach where bad things happen, R's limbs finally stopped trying to remember what to do and just moved. The beach tells her how to move.

Everything loose on her body was thrown into the wind, her hair skimmed K's cheek. K raised a hand to brush it off and looked over at R. "I'm not ready to leave yet."

A month later, she's yelling the same thing at R a little after 1 a.m. before K pushes off the wall and goes to the bathroom. R gives up on getting out of there at a decent hour and leaves her alone in order to scrounge for food at the bar. She rests her elbow against the counter, sticky enough that she can't slide. K treats her like shit because that's all she knows. The only friendships she has are ones centered around wanting to fuck each other. Well, them wanting to fuck her. Guys from their high school she would Skype late at night in her bedroom and whisper about the next day. R would sit backwards in her chair in the history class where they met, neglecting her notes and the friends she'd signed up for the class with. K doesn't know how to be a friend; she only knows how to convince someone to fall in love with her.

A few handfuls of peanuts later, R turns herself around and lays her eyes across the room. The lights peeling across the black of the dance floor, where bodies slide against each other's sweat. There's neon paint smeared along her right arm and she picks flakes of it off onto the ground as she tries to find K in the tangle. K has skin of black lace tonight, tight sleeves that keep her together, make her look small on top of the ripped-open jeans. Her hair is a bees' nest of wet and wasted, set in a sputter around her head. She rubbed acrylic paints in the ends of it in first-period art class on Friday, talking around the dark blue coffee cup to the guy who sat at her table and drew portraits of her every morning. There is yellow and pale green still hanging from the strands, color holding on to the far away parts of her.

She is waiting for R to move forward.

It is a beach where bad things happen. The tops of K's cheeks are damp and gray with makeup made foggy by the ocean. She holds onto R's hand, her fingers finding the scars on R's palm, smoothing them out like they would tell her where she came from. The trees lining the sand catch the tantrums of the waves and hold them in, turns them into knots and twists on their trunks.

One of the trash cans near them fall over in the wind, knocking plastic bags and beer cans across the sand. K's eyes startle. She looks past R toward the parking lot and bites salt off the edges of her lips.

"Humans—we're bad at loving," K says, rolling her sleeves up the freckles on her forearms. "We love selfish and jealous and mean. Love to death / love till death / love that kills." She sings it in an almost sing-song voice, rolling her eyes as she does so that R will know not to take her too seriously. She drops her voice again as she continues, mocking the tenor of their history teacher's lectures on adulthood as she instructs: "Be the person I fell in love with, but also be the person I am turning you into. The backbreaking pressure to become the things you love."

R feels the battered emerald of the trees behind her, how the strongest things are broken the most often.

It is a beach where bad things happen. Not bad enough to change your life, just bad enough to make R push a centimeter harder on the gas pedal as she and K start back down the road toward home that morning. They pass through the small town, all pie shops and bed-and-breakfasts. Families in red coats walking dogs with matching leashes, their noses deep in the neighbors' gardenias. A left turn at the stop sign and then straight on the one-lane road leading through the trees, their branches crab arms scuffling along the dunes on either side of the thin highway.

She glances at K, her knees pink against the coffee-stained passenger seat. R says, "I always lose to you."

"There's no such thing as winning." K slides a chipped fingernail along some of the glue on her skin, slowly peeling more and more of it up until she had a small continent of thin tissue.

She looks over at R's reflection in the rearview mirror and continues, "There's just living, moving forward. If you keep doing that, you'll be okay." She rolls down the window and drops dried glue onto the hills that pressed against the car from both sides.

R's skin feels worn down by wind; she's wearing a red flannel pulled on over a dry bathing suit. She feels the turns of the steering wheel all down her arms, the hairs picked up by the fabric as it stretches to make room for the hairpin snaking of the concrete.

On the last night the glue goes on easy. R knows to avoid the more tender skin on her upper thighs, learned on the nights K stripped the glue from her with her mouth. The glitter on K's knees glow under the lights of the club, twisting in R's eyes as she moves toward the wall where K stands, still in line for the bathroom.

And then another girl is between them, is stuck to the glue of K's thighs, laughing into her mouth.

It does not occur to R that she can break the rules until she does. She feels like she got the most obvious question on the test wrong. She peels off to the right before they see her, not that they would, now. Acid drags up R's throat as her fingers press against the soft pink of her insides. She thinks, absently, that her throat clenching around her fingers as she gags is just like the tightening inside of K when she is in the mood. She leans against the fence that lines the parking lot and imagines her fingers reduced to bone in her throat, imagines choking on them as they clink down her esophagus.

That, at least, would be a new pain.

It does not occur to her to wait for K. She is already in the car, already on the freeway back to her house and cold bed and parents who won't know what to do with her home. She is already ripping all of the stickiness from her legs and screaming into her cheek at the searing heat—*stay with the pain you're used to*.

K will pull away from the girl, will be tequila-furious at being left alone in the night, at this breaking of the rules—"if it was okay to leave without each other, I would've done that every fucking weekend."

R lays in bed, knowing that she will still show up the next morning. She worries that she will not know how to retort that she thought one of the rules was that they only kissed each other.

It was a beach where bad things happen. Not the kind of bad things you're thinking of. Bad like walking too far along the surf and missing your mother's calls to come home for dinner so that you grow one more day away from her. So when R got there on Sunday morning, early enough that the sky was the color of the peach fizz bikes they'd stolen a few weeks before, she looked around the parking lot an extra time, scanning the sand for something to hint this place was stuck in a space-time continuum she hadn't noticed yet. Half a crab scuttling towards the rocks, perhaps. Its body perfectly parallel to the ground in a feat defying any kind of gravity she'd ever known.

The waves pulled up across the sand like they were being spilled from a glass, and she watched the suds form along the horizon until her eyes went dry. Her toes were pickling in the damp sand as she headed out along the cliffs, their edges cascading with iceberg cactus that grabbed at the clay of the rocks holding up the parking lot. Metal trash cans bruised with rust and dents were collected in bushels every fifty yards or so as she walked.

Humans made redundancy dirty. It was perfectly normal in nature—necessary, even. Having just one of something meant that it could be wiped out more easily. You copy so that your kind can survive.

R got to the beach an hour before she was supposed to that final morning.

An hour before usual.

She didn't even know she was copying anymore, until she saw K's shoes at the edge of the parking lot.

The sun was a few inches off the water, the trees were dusty green along the rocks, and K was stripped down to nothing at the cut of the waves.

K moved forward always forward, afraid of leaving anything unknown.

The ocean was a gash across the horizon.

She walked right in.

ASH WEDNESDAY

Jennifer Abod

Sitting—two women
our favorite bench
outside St. Anthony's Church.

I'm in flip-flops.
Your brown hands
folding over the marble
topped cane, matches
pearly polish at your
fingers' tips.

On the sidewalk
children run, skip,
hold a parent or
grandparent's hand.

Handymen and caregivers
still in uniform
climb stone steps—
enter through
brown lacquered doors
under a turquoise arch.

Large murals
of a golden Jesus
glisten from above.

On the corner:
vendors sell tamales,
corn on a stick,

dried yellow fritters
in plastic bags.

I stand,
place my hands
on your shoulders,

kiss your lips.
Time slows.

Parishioners fill church steps;
big black crosses darken
children's foreheads.

Everyone has them!
I smile.
"Why you smiling?" you ask.

"I just kissed you—
on Ash Wednesday
in front of St. Anthony's Church."

Walking home,
we navigate the sidewalk—
the aroma of roasting corn;
Spanish in the air.

MIZ GILL

Amy Lauren

In the produce aisle, my teacher squints
as her partner holds a bag of grapes
against the fluorescent lights, both
sets of eyes scanning for bruises.
Skinny stripes on my teacher's wrists

flash in the white of the supermarket.
Before her eyes leave the grapes, I glance
away, grip the metallic handle of my cart
and steer down the aisle. I remember
the first time, in middle school,

she rolled up her sleeves to carry a stack
of papers. "Miz Gill, who hurt you?"
called a jock from the back. The black belt
framed on her desk suggested that
no one could hurt her. Yet the scars glared.

But, wheeling past the produce, I think
how she wears a short-sleeved blouse now;
they faded, those lines, visible
only in harsher light which exposes
every bruise, the oldest cut.

THERE I WAS IN ART SCHOOL

Suzanne Feldman

So, there I was in art school having a wonderful time, when I suddenly realized I had no job skills. I could draw and paint and sculpt, even weld with a gas torch, but none of that was going to make me any money. The year I graduated was 1981 and there was no internet, so I couldn't default to designing websites. After a few years of low-paying jobs, I did the only thing a little dyke without financial prospects could do: I put on a dress and applied to teach art in high school.

There were no jobs available in Baltimore, where I lived. The closest I could find was in rural Frederick County, Maryland, otherwise known as Fredneck. I ended up at Catoctin High School, an hour and fifteen minutes from my house—if I drove like a maniac. Which I did, for four years, because my wife, Vicki, had cancer and we couldn't afford to move.

Let me just say here that she's fine, knock on wood, it's thirty-some-odd years later and I've been retired for a while. Some things are just a blur, as they would be as time goes by, but there are some things I'll never forget.

My career in teaching pretty much spanned the arc of intolerance to grudging acceptance of Gay and Lesbian kids in school, at least in my area. Being a Lesbian teacher was a different story. In my first years of teaching, I wore skirts and dresses and desperately tried to grow my hair long. When I talked about my personal life at all, I talked about my husband. This worked for a while until one day, at the very end of my second year. The kids were mostly gone, and I was cleaning my room. I had a really big blackboard (not a whiteboard—back then we still used chalk) which I had erased completely. My erasers were dirty (there were maintenance issues, but that's a story for another time) and the whole board was dusty mess. I left to do something—pee?—and when I came back to my room, a kid was just walking out—a nice kid with curly blond hair whom I'd always liked. I wondered what he was doing there but didn't ask and kept cleaning. Quite a while later, I looked at the board. Someone had taken a damp rag and written DYKE in the chalk dust in huge letters. It barely showed, but at that point, I knew that that kid had done it, and my secret was out. I don't remember seeing him ever again, but as I did my hour-and-fifteen-minute drive home, first fearful, then mad, I finally came to the conclusion that it takes one to know one.

Afterwards, I applied the one-in-ten rule to my classes. If ten percent of the overall population is Gay, then surely that would apply even to a school out there in the sticks, where about two percent of the students didn't even have indoor plumbing, a significant number hunted deer for meat, and the KKK had its largest Eastern chapter. I looked and looked for these kids, wanting to protect them from harm and harassment, but I couldn't pick them out. I knew there were other Lesbian teachers in the county—my best friend was one—and there were at least two Gay men at Catoctin, but there was no solidarity, certainly no LGBT student group. There was nothing except a hug from a girl named Tonya, who, on the last day of my third year, threw her arms around my neck and sighed, "Oh, Ms. Feldman!" and I thought, Oh my god, it's *you!*

I was at Catoctin for seven years, and in that time I perfected my response to kids who would say things like "that's so gay." If I was within earshot, I would say, "so what you're saying is, 'that's so stupid.'" They would look confused, so I would go on.

Me: "So what you're saying is, Gay means stupid."

Kid: "I guess so."

Me: "So what you're saying is that Gay people are stupid, and when you say that, you're talking about hundreds of people you don't even know."

I would get interesting comebacks to this. First of all, I discovered that there were a lot of Gay uncles out there in Catoctin-land; but most of all, these kids had never been challenged on their choice of words. Things began to change. After a while, when I heard "that's so gay," all I had to say was "pick a different word," and they would. After a while they would correct each other. Every year I had to go through the same thing with new classes, but I felt like I was making progress until I butted up against the administration.

I had a kid in photography (I taught EVERYTHING in the arts) who cried. He was a sensitive soul, and I picked him out as a one-in-ten. I was afraid he was suicidal from the way he acted and from the way his worried girlfriend described him at home, and I went to the guidance department, as I was mandated to do, to tell them about him. They were sympathetic up until they asked why I thought he wanted to kill himself, and I told them, beating around the bush as well as I could, that he was probably Gay and had self-esteem issues. I could see the guidance counselor lose interest the minute he figured out what I was talking about. He just couldn't have given less of a shit. A suicide would mean one less Gay kid, and that was that. Fortunately, to the best of my knowledge, this unhappy boy did not kill himself, but it wasn't because he was getting help from the school.

Five years into my time at Catoctin, I became yearbook advisor, which meant I became a kind of queen. No one wanted to be yearbook advisor—it was a lot of work and a lot of late hours—but because a yearbook was a *necessity*, it gave me immunity from the petty whims of the principal. I was also free to choose the students who became my editors as opposed to every other class, from ceramics to Art One, where kids were thrown in because their schedules wouldn't accommodate anything else. Yearbook was special, and my classes were full of open-minded children. We did a yearbook edition with two pages devoted to

Elvis. In another one, when a Lesbian science teacher who was well-loved and respected was picked out and reprimanded for some stupid, forgettable thing, we did a multi-page spread on her honors and awards.

I have a lot of good memories from Catoctin, but I was glad to get out. I left for another school, Linganore High School, where I stayed for a year and a half before I was involuntarily transferred. Linganore was where my Lesbian friend and mentor Margaret taught and I thought I might be safer there, but no. Margaret was just as closeted as I was. The school was just as white-bread as Catoctin, though there was no Klan there.

In one class, a huge Art One with at least thirty students in it, I was targeted by parents. One girl, who threw pencils at me and thought she could get away with that, was a "daddy's girl" and told her parents that she thought I was a Lesbian. When I called home about the pencil-throwing, I got no results. Word spread quickly because all these kids played soccer together and their parents talked. I was blissfully unaware of this for a long time and thought I just had behavior problems in this ginormous class, and I kept making parent calls with little effect. It all became clear to me when my next-door neighbor Joe Davis, an elder statesman for the Boy Scouts, got a lifetime achievement award one night at the high-end venue of the Ceresville Mansion.

Vicki and I were seated at a table of honor with Joe's son, Jack, and the parents of this pencil-throwing girl, whose name I honestly forget. People had come to the ceremony from all over the world, all former Scouts who had worked with Joe and risen to high ranks, like the admiral of the American forces in Portugal. There were well over a hundred people. Joe got up behind the lectern and began thanking folks for being there. He started with Jack, and then thanked us. He was an elderly man at that point, and we did things like clean his gutters and rake his leaves. Joe said, "I'd like to thank Vicki and Suzanne for being here. They're young! They're energetic! They're—" He didn't say Lesbian, but the word was out there for anyone who wanted to see it. The mother of the girl who threw pencils just sent me an evil glare. She was *not* personally thanked, but Joe, a mover and shaker in the community that was Frederick County, had recognized *me*. And that was, more or less, the end of the behavior problems with her kid and that class. Wow, did I feel vindicated!

After that, I was transferred to Urbana High School, which was in the south of the county and closer to the DC metro area. By this time, we had moved to the City of Frederick, and the drive wasn't so bad. The school wasn't bad either. It was a brand-new building with a progressive principal who supported the arts, and there were four other art teachers there besides me. I was out to them, which felt great. The student body was racially mixed, which was a nice change, and after a couple of years, there was a *very* nascent LGBT student group.

It started in 1999 when a kid by the name of Jake came to me in a panic. He was looking for the LGBT club and he thought I was my friend Margaret who, though closeted, still had a reputation, on the internet at that point, for being open to "different" students. Jake had never been in my classes and never did take a class from me, but we became friends (and still are, on Facebook). His family situation was very bad, and he ran away from home in his senior year to become a street kid in Baltimore. (He found a wonderful man, married him, and is fine now.) He and his friend Kathy started the LGBT club, which I supported but couldn't lead. I was still afraid to come out to my students. There was, of course, some hostility to the LGBT club, and when we put up posters in my classroom, someone would tear them down—while class was in session. Finally, I got a video camera from the library, put it in a box with a peephole cut into it, and caught the culprit red-handed. The administration acted on it—a far cry from Catoctin—and the club meetings went on just like any other.

I took a year sabbatical after about eight years at Urbana and went to Johns Hopkins University to get a master's degree in creative writing in 2003. When I came back to teach, I had been transferred to Frederick High, about a mile from my house. Frederick High was considered an inner-city school because its population was mostly African American, but the fact was the school had such a diverse population that at least a dozen languages were spoken there, everything from Spanish to Urdu. Although I wasn't out at any of the schools I ever taught in, being a Lesbian seemed to matter less at Frederick High than anywhere else. There was always some sexual drama, though—the photo teacher was having sex in his office with the school secretary after hours, and so on—but I was never hassled or harassed by anyone because of my sexuality.

After a year at Frederick High I was sent back to Linganore, a place I had sworn I would never return to, but I didn't have a choice. It was that or quit teaching. There was a new principal, a woman, and I discovered that things had changed.

First of all, there was an LGBT club in full swing, led by a straight English teacher. I didn't have to be involved; I just needed to be supportive. Second, I became the very cool teacher who brought her dog to school once a week. Gracie was a pound rescue. With me, she was certified for visiting nursing homes, with a card and everything. I'd bring her in on Wednesdays, and the kids loved it. They would compete to be the one who took her outside to pee. Having her there gave the classroom a whole different feel, like a home instead of an institution of learning. Kids who were problems for other teachers came to my class to pet the dog. She was a huge hit with special education, and my art classes became this island of love and dogginess. I still run into former students who ask me about her.

I was at Linganore for many years. The original building had to be torn down, and as a school we moved around the county for two years until the replacement was built. With the new building came a new principal, a Gay man, who didn't like me and hated the whole idea of having a dog in school. He was unmarried, lived with his father, and had a pretty "fey" attitude, but his was an old county name, and he'd been in the system for as long as I had. So there he was, in a position of power, unhassled, hassling me. I was a target again, this time in the sights of a person whom I had taught with at Catoctin and Urbana and had had as a vice principal at Linganore—I mean we had history together. It took me a long time to get my mind around the fact that his ultimate goal was to get rid of me, and get rid of me he did, sending me halfway across the county to Tuscarora High School.

At this point, I was a twenty-four-year veteran of the Frederick County Public Schools and closing in on retirement. I had no intention of being closeted with my new colleagues and they were very welcoming. I was still not out to the kids, but now I was two decades past skirts and long hair. I was wearing tie-dye shirts, jeans, and a short haircut, and my kids just made their own assumptions. I was accepted and never bothered by students or parents, and the out students were very straightforward with me. The administration didn't care, and, aside from a few ridiculous behavior problems involving kids watching *Orange Is the New Black* on their cellphones during class, I enjoyed my time at Tuscarora.

Now, after a few years of retirement and especially after writing this essay, I look back and see how far we have come, and yet how fragile our gains are as LGBT folk. I was not teaching when forty-five took office, but I know his election emboldened kids who tended to the hater side of politics, and I'm sure that made a difference to the LGBT clubs at the county's schools. In some ways, I wish I could go back to protect those communities. In some ways, I'm glad I'm not there. At this point in my life I might end up just slapping someone.

On the other hand, as I sent this essay out to be read by former colleagues and former students, I found that, even as closeted as

I was, I was pretty obvious to some. A girl who's a young woman now wrote that she knew I was a Lesbian but never said anything about it to anyone because she wanted to "protect me from all that teenage bullshit." Jake tells me I saved his life. Teachers in the system tell me that Frederick County Public Schools have reached beyond the school-by-school LGBT club to mandatory staff development on LGBTQ students and staff. Obviously, this won't change the narrow-minded views of some, but every teacher has gotten professional development to learn about gender identity and sexuality. The new policies are being challenged in court, but that challenge is being fought by students who, twenty years ago, might've been too frightened to come out and help themselves.

In the end, it does amaze me how far we've come as a society in the span of my teaching career. I never, ever thought I'd get to legally marry my wife, but here I am, thirty-five years into a relationship that was legalized in 2010. No matter how far back we are pulled by this insidious right-wing wave, the one-in-ten are still out there, teaching, learning, getting married, having children, having careers, and influencing society.

We still have a long way to go, but I have learned to be optimistic.

LEARNING ON THE JOB

sb sōwbel

We saw her letting
    the manager
of the whole cleaning staff
    hump her like a dog.

We knew she'd made the choice,
    to get a day off
    to be with her kid.

Still, it's hard to watch submission
    even if we know we're all
    bodies of compromise
Still, it's those fire-eaters with their iron throats
    and circus of self-invention
    to get to places blocked
Still, crackling and extinguishing flames
    at the same time, they,
    like Mary, manage to
    choose and control
    though these choices
    also, at once extinguish
    and burn.

This learning on the job
This is applied knowledge

breaks
any thinking heart
by degrees.

MEMORIAL HILL

Elizabeth Galoozis

Young and fervent in a planted valley,
we spouted impulse from our pens,
our green fingers. Our words meant
everything. Each other's words.
Every word. We thumped tutorial
tables, pulled books free
from library shelves together.
I danced, watched others dance,
watched you dance like you never told me
your trouble. I shouldered you home, only
a little less drunk than you. You said
you wished you could give me more.

Light and dark rushed in where we let them.
Time pushed us, green and fighting,
to parse harsh words at distance.
I framed the green, the gold, tossed
you in with the rest I buried. Our words
meant everything. Each other's words,
syllables already calcified.

You and I followed time
into grace, into each other's
graces. The grass, the monuments,
the pages, lost their sharpness
in receding. Over
our first post-reconciliation
call, you relate how
you drank whiskey
at the White Horse Tavern,

strutted home chanting
"Dylan Thomas, motherfuckers,
Dylan Thomas!" Poor
Dylan Thomas, slipping
unconscious into legend,
mourning his youth
a final time. We
are only thirty, our words
more polished every year.
Stumbling from the street,
but stumbling forward.

THE BRANCHES REGARD THE TREE

Elizabeth Galoozis

You began with impromptu lessons
about acceptable mates, pointing out
the car window: no tattoos,
no smoking, no one like *that*.
(Like what?)
Later, oblique rules
meant as barricades:
keep my door open
and my feet on the floor.
Be home by eleven;
only sleep over
with other girls.

I thought it was all mine
to unmake.
The relief of splitting
from conviction mine to feel,
sliding into a backseat
under my own supervision.

But you hemmed yourself in, too.
Gave in to painful
ramifications.
I didn't grow away
fast enough, didn't predict
the dissonant crack across the limbs
that was always coming.

GUITAR WOMAN

Sarah Pritchard

You sent me to learn the guitar
because I was the son you didn't have
to copy Grandfather's way
I played it until I let it go
rebelling the wrong way round.

But the woman playing a guitar
still struck chords in me that
resounded me into a first kiss
with another woman who said we stood
with our arms like
we were playing guitars.

The metronome is ticking right now
counting me down . . . 3 . . . 2 . . . 1 . . .
how many more heartbeats before
I pick up the woman-shaped instrument
to make music again?

SUNDAY MORNING

Shelonda Montgomery

I'm going to ask her to be my girlfriend, Abby thinks to herself as she looks through a dirty church window. Anna Benton, the pastor's daughter, sits alone on a church pew rehearsing her lines for the junior choir's youth revival performance. *Okay*, Abby thinks. She looks at her trembling hands and closes her eyes tight. Doubt paralyzes her. She thinks the two locked eyes a few times. Thinks she saw Anna smile at her. Anna Benton is the prettiest girl at Holy Saints Missionary Baptist Church. All of the boys like her and follow her around and the congregation dotes on her because she is proper, well-mannered, polite, and a straight-A student.

"What if it's just me?" Abby says to herself. She opens her eyes and, again, stares into the small window. Her dirty black high-top Chuck Taylor gym shoes are pressed into the dirt. Her beige flowery dress hangs below her knees and flows with the wind. As she moves, her dress brushes her white, red-trimmed tube socks that Cissy, her grandmother, instructed her not to wear. She hates dresses but wears them because Cissy makes her. However, she resolves, to herself only, to keep the socks. *This dress would look good on Anna Benton*, Abby thought to herself as she dressed this morning. Anna wears pinks and yellows and oranges and to Abby, Anna smells like honey or freshly cut sugarcane.

"Abigail, get over here!" Cissy now says.

Abby runs to Cissy who looks down at her pointedly. "What are you doing over there? You know these people don't want you in they flowers." Abby looks back at the crushed lilies in the dirt, her shoe print between them. She runs over and tries to fix them as much as she can, holding a lumpy lily in her hands as if she is a surgeon trying to restore life to it. "*Girl*, get over here!"

Cissy says. Abby lets the lily go and walks to her grandmother. The lily, weathered and tired, slowly returns to the dirt and nuzzles itself within the shoeprint. Anna Benton closes her hymnbook and sings her verse. The beatific sound echoes through the small church and seeps through the windows and door crevices like fog searching about the air.

"Why don't she ever sit with us?" Robert says to Abby. From the church's second-floor balcony they look down at Anna, who stands onstage with the director and members of the junior choir.

"Don't know." Several members of the choir prepare to sing.

"She is so pretty," Robert says and wipes his sweaty brow.

Abby places her hands on the cold railing, leans over, stretches her neck like an ostrich searching for food, and looks at Anna again. "She Okay."

"Okay. . . no. She more than Okay. She pretty."

"If you think so."

"I do. You think she'll be my girlfriend if I ask her?"

"Nope." Abby presses her face against the bars, her heart in her stomach at the thought of someone liking Anna. *And Robert. Not Robert. Robert. Robert is not good for Anna*, she thinks.

"You *don't* think she'll be my girlfriend?"

"Noooooooooooooo."

"Why you say that?"

"Because she the pastor's daughter and the pastor ain't gone let her be your girlfriend. And she ain't cute anyway. You should ask Hattie Cowan to be your girlfriend."

Robert frowns. "Hattie Cowan?"

"What's *wrong* with Hattie Cowan?" Abby says, her hand on her hip as if she is her grandmother telling off a clerk, or waitress, or someone somewhere who did not give her all of her change.

Robert scratches his head. "Hattie Cowan is okay, but she ain't no Anna." Hattie Cowan has huge glasses and is often referred to as homely by the neighborhood children, including Robert.

"*Boy*, Anna *ain't* cute and you crazy if you *think* she is."

"What she do to you?"

Abby picks up her backpack, runs down the balcony stairs, and leaves out of a side door. Robert grabs his backpack and follows her.

"Where you going?" he asks, running behind her.

"Home," she says, pointing to her house in the distance beyond a field of brush.

"Why you going home?"

"'Cause my grandmamma told me to be home by dinner and it's almost dinner."

"Oh. can I go?"

"Nope."

"Come on, why? I love your grandmamma's cooking."

Abby sharpens her eyes like knives at Robert.

"Come on, Abby."

"Nope. Bye, Robert," she says, places one of the straps of her backpack on her shoulder, and stomps like a soldier around the field, creating dust clouds that twirl and spin at her feet.

"What took you so long to get home?" Cissy says, standing at the kitchen sink, drying a plate and looking at Abby.

Abby places her backpack on a kitchen chair. "Had to stop by the church." She takes a cup from the rack, opens the refrigerator, and pours herself a cup of fruit punch.

"Right . . . You *did* tell me a few days ago that you were going to the church and would be home late. Did you like it?"

"No."

"Why not?"

"'I don't want to be in it, Grandma. I hate singing."

"Pastor said it would be good for you. Said it'll help you adjust to being out here."

I don't want to adjust, Abby thinks, staring into her cup as if in a trance.

"I want to go back home with my momma, Grandma," she says, her voice low.

"I know, but she sent you to live down here until she gets things situated." "Just try it, Abigail," Cissy says, her eyes low and voice soft, as if pained by Abby's resistance to joining the junior choir. "It's a nice choir and the children are so sweet. And that little Anna. She is the nicest little thing. Sweet as a peach." Abby looks at the linoleum-tiled floor and allows her eyes to trace the boxes. "It's just hard now," Cissy continues, "because it's new to you. Can you just try it for a little longer?"

Abby nods.

"And maybe if all goes well, the pastor will give you a solo someday. That would be so nice, wouldn't it?" Cissy says, smiling.

"What's that I smell?" Abby's grandfather Earl, recovering from a stroke, slowly walks into the kitchen. He grabs the top of a chair and tries to sit down but nearly falls. Cissy quickly grabs him and helps him into the chair.

"Oxtail stew, cabbage, and dressing," Cissy says. "I told you I would bring your meal."

Earl takes a piece of tissue out of his pocket and wipes his hands and forehead, ignoring her. Cissy looks at him and frowns. "You couldn't wait, huh?"

Earl tries to adjust himself in the chair.

"Do you want to eat in here or do you want me to take it in the room? I can set it on your TV tray and you can watch TV and eat," Cissy says.

Earl moves from side to side in the chair and stops. "Well. I'm here now, so I'll just eat it here." He sucks his teeth a little and tries to secure a loose denture with his tongue. Abby stands and absentmindedly flicks a piece of plastic hanging from her cup.

"Okay." Cissy takes a bowl from the rack. "Earl, Abby joining the choir," she says, as if she just remembered to tell him and is afraid she might forget.

"Why you got her joining that shit?" Earl frowns as if he just smelled a foul odor.

Sissy spins around so fast that she stumbles. "Earl! Stop all that! I got her joining the choir because it's good for her."

Earl fans his hand, his forearm resting on the back of the chair.

"Earl, stop. It is a good church. The pastor is nice . . . he's a good man. The congregation is, too . . . Abby, go upstairs and clean up for dinner," Cissy says.

"Yes, ma'am," Abby says, grabs her backpack, and runs upstairs.

Holy Saints Missionary Baptist Church is small and wooden, yet beautiful. Its steeple is high and its windows are lined with stained glass. It is packed every Sunday morning for service and every Wednesday night for Bible study. Now Sunday service has just ended, and the congregation stands in fellowship greeting each other, eating cake and pie, and drinking tea and coffee. The church's elders made peach cobblers and display them proudly on tables.

"Keep us, Lord," Anna sings softly, sitting and swinging her legs on a bench behind the church and holding a sheet of song lyrics. She stops singing, unfolds the paper, and reads the lyrics. She stands and walks down a dirt path, holding the paper behind her back, slipping and moving it between her fingers. "Through the storm. Through the night," she sings. Suddenly, just as she takes a step, a black snake slithers across her path and nearly brushes her shoe. Anna screams and runs behind a tree. Abby sprints forward and grabs the snake. It wriggles in her small hand and struggles to break free. Holding the snake, Abby proudly walks over to Anna.

"Just a snake," Abby says, holding the snake out to Anna. Anna frowns and turns her head away. Abby throws it into the grass and wipes her hands on her dress, which is two sizes too large. "It wasn't poisonous," she says, rubbing her hands together as if trying to remove the remaining dirt.

"How do you know?" Anna asks, looking at Abby pointedly and studying the crooked ponytail sitting atop her frizzy, sandy-brown hair and the smudge of dirt on her cheek that looks as if it has been there for some time.

"'Cause it was not. I know snakes. Use to see them all the time when I use to go fishing."

"What are you doing out here anyway?" Anna asks.

Abby looks down.

Sister Gene, an usher, peeks her head out of the back door, looks at Abby, and frowns. Behind her the choir sings. Abby tries to smooth her hair and brushes dirt off her dress. Wearing a pink floral dress, Anna stands and balances her white purse on her bent wrist. Her hair is shiny and not a strand is out of place, the neatly combed baby hair greased and curled. Her lips have a coat of fresh pink gloss and her nails a matching coat of fresh pink polish. Her face is oiled, which makes her dark umber skin looks as if it is glowing, complementing her big, bright, delicate almond eyes and long eyelashes. She smells like strawberries because she habitually dabs strawberry perfume behind her ears and on her wrists.

"Anna, come inside," Sister Gene says. Anna walks inside. Abby follows her.

Anna stands onstage in the center of the choir and sings during rehearsal. The junior choir joins in and follows her lead. Abby stands in the far back corner as if hidden. She peeks out from behind the drums and taps her dirty sneakers. Overwhelmed by the rhythm, she starts singing. The choir director squints his eyes and puffs his cheeks. He then pushes his eyeglasses down a little and looks over the rim at Abby, who puts her hands over her mouth and slowly rocks from side to side. The choir director takes Abby by the hand, guides her to a pew, and sits her down.

The sun is setting, and members of the congregation walk toward their cars. Abby walks alone on a dirt road toward home, her head down. She walks slow and drags her backpack by her side as if it is full of stones.

"Hey, thanks for saving me today!"

Abby turns around and sees Anna standing in the middle of the road.

"I ain't save you. I told you that snake wasn't going to kill you."

"But still . . . Thanks." Anna looks down at the ground, up, and around. "Can you help me sell some gift baskets this Saturday? We have to raise money for the junior choir. My father said if I sell them, people will line up to buy them. Can you help me?"

Abby nods.

Anna smiles. "Thank you. I'll tell sister Gene. Meet me here at 11 a.m. on Saturday."

Abby fidgets with her dress. "Okay."

Anna runs back into the church. Abby rushes home, smiling the entire way and clutching her backpack to her chest as if it were a sack of weightless feathers.

"Mr. Hudson, how are you on this beautiful Saturday morning?" Anna says, standing at Mr. Hudson's doorstep. She is in a white lace dress with matching gloves and holds a gift basket. Abby stands in the distance, peeking around a tree.

Mr. Hudson's eyes light up. "Anna Benton, what brings you by this Saturday morning? How's your grandmother doing?"

"She's quite well, thank you," Anna says, smiling and partially curtsying.

"And the pastor?"

"My father is well also, sir."

"Mildred!" Mr. Hudson leans back and yells into the house. "Anna Benton, Elder Benton's granddaughter, is at the door!"

"Really!" a voice yells from within the house. "Well now!" In moments, Mr. Hudson's wife stands at the door, smiling. "Anna!" she says, then runs off the porch and hugs Anna.

Anna looks back and smiles at Abby. "You look so nice." Mildred continues, "I was *just* talking to the pastor about you. I told him that he should be so proud of the little lady that you've become."

Anna blushes and looks down. "Thank you, Mrs. Hudson. That means so much."

"And I love your bow," Mildred says, patting a lace bow that delicately sits on Anna's head. "How is your grandmother?"

"She is fine, Mrs. Hudson. How are you?"

"Fine, fine, Anna. I'm fine . . . you are so polite. Isn't she, Henry?"

"She is," Henry says, smiling.

"What brings you by, Anna?" Mildred asks.

"We are selling gift baskets to raise money for the junior choir," Anna says as she walks over to a red wagon and uncovers a bag of elaborately made gift baskets.

Mrs. Hudson eyes light up. "Look at that! Beautiful!"

"Mr. and Mrs. Hudson, as you know, we have a youth revival coming up and we—"

"No need to say anything else, Anna!" Mrs. Hudson says, extending her arm and shaking her head. "We will take four . . . no . . . give me about five. I'll give some to the ladies at the hospital. They will love them! They love little cute stuff like this."

"They bought five?" Abby asks, pulling the wagon.

"Yep." Anna counts the money and rolls it tight as they walk down a trail. "Okay, now it's your turn," she says and looks at a huge house sitting regally on a hill.

Abby swallows hard. "That's a big house."

"It is. Which means they have money . . . and we need money. Come on." Anna beckons for Abby to follow her and starts walking up the hill. They arrive at the front door. "Stand right here," Anna says and hides behind a tree. Abby looks around, rubs her hair to try to fix strands sticking up, and rings the doorbell. Dr. Miller opens the door slowly. He pokes his nose out.

"Hhhhhhhhheeeeellllllllllllooo," Abby says, stuttering so much that she spits, and it splatters like rain.

Dr. Miller frowns. "What?" he asks, his voice husky.

"Hhhhelllllloooo, dddddddddddo doo dddddddddddddo you want to buy some gift baskkketss Mr.," Abby says, fidgeting with the rim of her dress so much that her rolled up, red-trimmed tube socks and muddy high-top gym shoes show.

"What!"

"Who is that!" a woman yells from inside the house.

Dr. Miller looks around the door. "I think it's Cissy's granddaughter. You know, the one she took in because the mother fell on hard times." The woman comes to the door and looks at Abby. She then looks at the uncovered gift baskets. The covering hangs and lies partially on the concrete. Abby quickly rushes over and tries to fix the covering.

She looks up at the couple."Dddddo yyyyou wwwwwantt to buy—"

"No, baby. We don't want none of them baskets," Mrs. Miller says, frowning. Abby drops her head, takes the wagon and walks away. The wagon crashes against rocks and debris, making a loud clucking sound.

"That was good," Anna says, waiting beside the tree.

Abby sits on a log and picks up a stick.

Anna looks at her, her face somber. "It was good."

"They like you," Abby whispers, her eyes red and watery.

"They *don't* like me. They like my grandmother and father. Everybody likes them, so they think they like me."

Abby, sitting with her head down, peels a piece of bark from the stick, and throws it to the ground.

"Is that true what he said about your mother?" Anna asks, her voice soft. Abby rubs the stick between her fingers. Anna stands directly in front of her. "Stand up." Abby stands. They are so close that their noses almost touch. Anna takes a tissue from her purse and wipes smudge marks from Abby's chin and forehead. "Here, take off your jacket." Abby removes her leather jacket, her dress wrinkled and dusty. "Pat your dress off." Abby starts whacking her dress. "No, like this," Anna says and starts wiping and patting Abby's dress. Anna takes her brush out of her purse and brushes the front of Abby's hair. "Turn around, please," Anna says. Abby turns around and Anna takes strands of Abby's hair, which are sticking up, rubs them down, puts the hair into a ponytail, and takes the lace bow from her head and places it on Abby's. In order to inspect her work, she again faces Abby. Anna smells like strawberries and her lips are slick with freshly applied gloss. Abby's heart beats and she begins to sweat.

"Now, let's try this again," Anna says and looks at a house in the distance. "Here, put this on." She takes out her lip gloss, applies it to Abby's lips, and rubs it in with her pinky finger. "Okay, come on. We'll do it together this time." She takes Abby's hand in hers and feels that it is covered in sweat. "Are you nervous?" Abby looks at her, wipes her brow and nods. Anna looks into Abby's eyes. "I am too." She squeezes Abby's hand and holds it tight. They walk down the hill and ring the doorbell. The door creaks as it opens.

Anna sits in church inside the choir box. She sees Abby and Cissy walk in, so she rubs her hair back and sits up straight.

Abby and Cissy sit in a pew. Pastor Benton is preaching. Abby opens her Bible and looks at Anna.

"What are you doing?" Cissy says when she sees that Abby did not turn to Matthew 3:17 as Pastor Benton instructed.

Abby looks up at her grandmother. "Nothing."

Cissy stares at Abby's open Bible. "He said Matthew 3:17."

Abby starts flipping through the pages, trying to find the scripture. Anna stares at her. Their eyes meet and Abby looks away, smiles, and turns to Matthew 3:17.

"How are you liking that choir?" Cissy asks, sweeping the front porch.

Abby rests her body on the fence, leaning over it. "It's okay."

"Just okay? Either you like it, or you don't . . . *Girl*, move and let me get over here," she says, sweeping beside Abby's feet and trying to sweep the spot where Abby is standing. "It is a good church. There are some good kids in that choir. That reminds me . . . y'all youth revival is coming up this Sunday. The junior choir is going to sing, right?"

Abby nods.

"Are you ready?" Cissy asks.

Abby, again, nods.

"Okay. If not, just practice. Go over the lines that you don't know. Do you like the dress I got you?"

Abby puffs her jaw and releases the air slowly, balancing herself on the edges of her gym shoes, and slouches on the fence, her arms dangling like tired, wreathed willow tree branches. "It's okay," she says, as if she just remembered to respond.

"The pastor told me to get you there early, so we gone get dressed and be on our way, okay?"

"Okay, Abby says and moves her feet. Cissy sweeps in the desired spot.

A stage is set up outside behind the church and long tables with white linens line the lawn. The parishioners wait to hear the junior choir sing.

"I hate ham and they always serve ham at these things. Ham . . . and luncheon meat that is often passed off as ham," Anna says to Abby. They are dressed in white and stand in a food line beside a table covered in dishes in plastic containers or huge aluminum trays that have Chafing Dish Fuel and a PowerPad underneath. The dishes are macaroni and cheese, ham, gumbo, collard greens, macaroni salad, potato salad, coleslaw, fried chicken, two cakes, and two peach cobbler pies. Anna skips the ham and dips a huge spoon in a coleslaw container and places some onto her plate, which has potato salad and macaroni salad on it.

Abby looks at the ham. "I like it." She puts a piece on her plate. "This all my Grandma ever cooks."

"Is your mom coming to see you perform?" Anna asks.

Abby shakes her head and struggles to place a roll on her plate, her eyes low. Anna looks at her. "I'm sure she will get a chance to stop by and see you soon."

"I told you to come by my house and get me!" Robert says, running up to Abby. He is dressed in white, his face is shiny, and his hair is neat and extra oily, as if someone forgot to rub the oil in properly.

Abby spins around to Robert. "I told you that if me and my grandmother was running late we were going to go on to church."

Robert shakes his head.

"Hi Anna," he says, staring at Anna as if he just realized she is standing there.

"Hi Robert," Anna says and smiles.

"Abby, are you ready to sing in the choir today?" Robert asks, his voice trembling as if he could not think of anything else to say to Anna.

"I am," Abby says.

"How are you, Robert?" Anna says.

Robert blushes and smiles. "Fine," he says and nervously twirls a strand of his oily hair between his fingers. "How are you, Anna?" He rubs the back of his head, looks down, and kicks a rock, grinning.

"I am very well, thank you, Robert." With her tray in her hand, Anna looks around. "Where do you want to sit, Abby?"

Abby looks at an empty corner table. "Over there."

Abby and Anna walk to the empty table. Just as Anna positions herself to sit down beside Abby, Robert runs up and sits between them, a leg on both sides of the bench.

"So . . ." he says, opening a bag of potato chips, "Abby, do you know the whole song?"

"I think so," Abby says. "I was working on it all night. My grandma said she would help me but fell asleep . . . but I think I know it."

"But do you know the *whole* song?" Robert says, stuffs a chip into his mouth, and starts crunching loudly.

Anna stands up, throws out her food, and walks away, her shoulders straight and chin up high.

"Why she do that?" Robert says.

Abby looks at Anna, then back to Robert, and shrugs.

"Why you throw your food away?" Abby says.

Anna stands inside the kitchen in front of the refrigerator, holding a wrapped food dish.

"I have to get this back out there. Sister Gene told me to get it and come right out because people are waiting," Anna says.

"Are you mad at Robert?" Abby asks, as if Anna had not said a word. Anna shakes her head. "Why you throw your food away then?"

"Why did you have to talk to him?"

"He my friend."

"I thought you were going to talk to me."

"Anna!" Sister Gene yells into the kitchen.

"Coming!" Anna closes the refrigerator door.

"Give me that," Sister Gene says, rushing into the kitchen. She takes the dish out of Anna's hands. "I told you to come right out," she says, walking wide with the food dish and making sure that its contents do not spill on her. "Come on in here."

Anna follows Sister Gene. She looks back at Abby who stands with her eyes wide and mouth open, her hand on the refrigerator.

"Holy, holy, Lord," Anna, wearing a white choir robe, sings. She is alone on stage. "He is my comfort through the storm. Holy, holy, Lord."

"Holy!" the other members of the choir sing, including Abby, who sings with her eyes closed.

Anna rocks slowly. "Keep me, lead me home . . . through the night." Anna walks in front of the other choir members and stands.

The choir, in unison, clap their hands and stomp their feet. The organist, pianist, and drummers play, enhancing the choir. The congregation joins in and all jubilantly sing, dance, and perform in unison. The celebration is heard miles away in neighboring towns. Abby opens her eyes and smiles at Anna, who smiles back.

Abby picks up a rock and throws it into the river. She wipes her hands on her robe.

"Sister Gene is going to get you if you get your robe dirty," Anna says, holding a glass of water.

"It's already dirty," Abby says, patting at a dirt stain. Anna sits beside Abby on the rock and sips from her glass. Abby stares at her.

"What," Anna says, taking the cup from her mouth. Abby leans over and kisses her. Anna jumps up and drops the glass, which shatters at her feet. She then wipes her lips with the back of her hand, spits on the ground, and walks back to the church, spitting as she walks. From the rock, Abby watches Anna walk into the church. Within moments, several members of the congregation pile out and stare at Abby, who sits frozen. In time, a crowd forms, stands, and stares at Abby. Anna stands in the middle of the crowd drinking water, wiping her mouth with the back of her hand, and spitting, her white robe rippling and flowing in the wind. Abby runs into the field, her white, dirt-stained robe disappearing into the brush.

BILLIE

Gloria Keeley

Thelonious played Black Crow
low and slow
strange fruit still echoes
blackened in the cold hard sun

night fell on
the slip knot of moon
color lines drawn on
the maps of trees
roots unaware
magnolias budded white
sway with the gentle breeze

music of washboards and harps
far from plantation mansions
in the backwater's dark strut
with the taps of shoes
before the wolves hunt
the black locusts buzz

gospel singers tune
their collective voices
the fruit gathered neatly
beneath the darkening shade
headed toward heaven
the horns blow Dixie

JANIS JOPLIN, WE MISS YOU

Gloria Keeley

For Pearl

When I think of Pearl
and where she's lying, I go crazy
When I think of Pearl
and how she's burning, I go mad

> She's into black, magical indulgence
> She's into mysterious mind fusions

I'm scared to go too near her swirling vortex
I'm scared to try to touch her troubled brain
I'm scared of cerebral pains that can't be lifted
I'm scared of scarred emotions, blood-teared rain

When I think of Pearl
and how she's dying, I can't think right, I can't think right
When I think of Pearlie Pearl
and how she's crying, I can't sleep

> She's out of touch with everyone that's in her
> She's out of touch with all contained outside

To calm her
I'll make bracelets of the moon
To calm her
I'll paint skies inside her eyes
To calm her
I'll put her somewhere with a flower

To stop her
I'll keep her safe within my smile

(Like when night comes and there's enough riverwood
for her fire.)

I (STILL) WANT A WOMEN'S (AND LESBIAN FEMINIST) REVOLUTION

Wendy Judith Cutler

Feminism has always been about resistance to me. Being a lesbian and a feminist means I will always resist all forms and manifestations of oppression as I envision a world of liberation. I have always preferred the term "women's liberation movement" because it is true to its radical, at the root, origins and its connections to other liberatory movements that it either came from or spawned.

As an open and out Jewish lesbian feminist since turning twenty-one in 1973, I have lived resistance. We lived in a universe that never recognized us, to which we were basically invisible or marginalized and, if acknowledged, only critically and negatively. I could never have survived without resisting any number of things: conformity, heterosexist and sexual norms, and the pressures of patriarchal culture and society. This was despite my class, race, and educational privileges, which meant that those without these privileges were even more vulnerable and punished by the interlocking systems of oppression.

If the women's liberation movement had not availed itself to me, I may never have discovered this path. Lesbian feminism embodied resistance and was an almost natural progression from my hippie-radical-feminist-socialist identities. Despite rejection from my parents, the larger culture, and world, I felt proud to be part of this movement for change and transformation. My life would never be the same and neither would it be for thousands upon thousands of us. And for that I am full of gratitude.

When I was twenty-one, I discovered Robin Morgan's poetry book, *Monster*, which I purchased at A Woman's Place Bookstore in Oakland, California, the first feminist bookstore in North America. I had already devoured the essays and stories in *Sisterhood is Powerful*, edited by Morgan, the first women's liberation anthology many of us found searching for feminist inspiration in the early 1970s.

Morgan's poem, "I Want a Women's Revolution" begins:

> I want a women's revolution like a lover.
> I lust for it, I want so much this freedom,
> this end to struggle and fear and lies
> we all exhale, that I could just die
> with the passionate uttering of that desire.
> (Robin Morgan. *Monster.* New York: Vintage Books, 1972)

I read this aloud to myself in my upstairs bedroom in the collective women's household I shared with three other women on Hillegas Street in a small brown cottage behind the main residence on a tree-lined Berkeley neighborhood south of campus. We had moved to the cottage from another house on the corner of Grant and Hearst, across from what was then known as People's Park Annex, which I frequented with my dog, Djuna.

It was called that during the People's Park uprising that erupted in the spring of 1969 when the university decided to turn an empty lot, which was being used as a community park, into a parking lot. The playground equipment, benches, and free box were brought there during the National Guard occupation.

I, too, wanted a revolution, craved change, real change. I had read about earlier revolutions in China, in Cuba, in some Latin American and African countries, but none of these were spearheaded by women, even though women were definitely part of these transformations and served as inspirations to many of us. Then I read about women's herstories and the plethora of publications of all kinds about this women's revolution, lesbian liberation that would radically alter how we think of everything. I, too, lusted for this sisterhood.

> Just once in this my only lifetime to dance
> all alone and bare on a high cliff under cypress trees
> with no fear of where I place my feet.
> To even glimpse what I might have been and never never
> will become, had I not had to waste my life fighting
> for what my lack of freedom keeps me from glimpsing
> (*Monster*)

Truthfully, in looking back, I didn't know what I was up against. Had I known, I may have prematurely surrendered. I was not raised to be a rebel of any sort. I was unprepared for the battle I would be waging against my upbringing, my biological family, requirements and restrictions, what seemed like the entire world.

Possibilities emerged as never before. Rebellion glowed in the foreground. I was so carried away by the passions and purposes of this women's, and later lesbian feminist, revolution.

I had tasted the sweet nectar of resistance. Women soon became my world, my sustenance, my passion. I joined an anti-rape collective and was falling in love with my best friend.

Bay Area Women Against Rape (BAWAR) was founded in 1971 by two activist feminists, the first rape crisis center in North America. I joined the collective in 1973. During my first anti-rape collective meeting, I sat in a circle on the floor with fifteen other women, some lesbians, some straight, some bi-sexual, mostly young, college-educated, and white. I had never been to a meeting like this, but had secretly, even from myself, yearned for this: a circle of women, a sisterhood. Luck and feminist activism brought me to this collective of women. I found my place among women working for change, changing the laws, changing our lives, changing other women's lives we hoped, we visioned. This is the political yet very personal work of feminism, this women's liberation movement.

> It is the primacy of women relating to women, of women creating a new consciousness of and with each other which is at the heart of women's liberation and the basis for the cultural revolution.... As we feel this growing solidarity with our sisters
>
> From Radicalesbians, "The Woman-Identified Woman" in *Women: A Journal of Liberation,* Winter 1971.

Once I started to be part of this anti-rape collective, I saw rape everywhere. Violence was perpetrated against women without regard to age, race, class, education, or sexuality. As soon as I recognized that rape existed everywhere and it served as a warning, punishment, an aspect of control and power to keep women down and in their subordinate places, I understood what was meant by the need for a complete transformation of society.

This living rape and embodying feminism was enthralling and also taking its toll, a rollercoaster dynamic of highs and lows. Embracing feminism meant continual awareness of sexism, not theoretically but personally. The meetings I sat through, my shifts on the rape crisis line, the radical classes I was taking, the books I was reading—all of it added more fuel to my anger at the misogynistic world I lived in. There was no escaping the conspiracies foisted on women. I wondered if it would ever stop.

While I may not have understood everything about the significance of placing myself on the floor in this particular meeting, I was joining this collective, this movement of women. I felt solidarity with many other movements, collectives, projects, and organizations that were resisting many forms of oppression. I understood the need for major transformation in order for any real change to occur in our lives, our laws, our relationships, our futures. I truly believed this, and it is still my vision of this world that we are trying to change. While I was not ready to join the underground and pledge commitment to a militant organization,

I felt a sense of connection with those who occupied the radical fringes of these revolutionary movements.

When a small package arrived when I opened the door of the BAWAR office to begin my shift, I was surprised. The package had been hand-delivered, not mailed, and was a red soft-covered, over-sized book titled *PRAIRIE FIRE: The Politics of Revolutionary Anti-Imperialism, Political Statement of the Weather Underground*. On the title page were written the words: "Printed Underground in the U.S. For the People" with the Weather Underground insignia and its dedication to "Harriet Tubman and John Brown; to all who continue to fight; to all political prisoners in the U.S." I brought the book home to my household, and we sat on the porch reading aloud to each other. Inside we read the words from "The Rising of Women":

> . . . rape—a massive, brutal system of terror perpetrated on women by men . . . The oppression of women perverts the cultural values of the whole society . . . The women's movement has reached into every home, awakening women's potential and challenging our subjugation . . . Lesbianism has been an affirmation of unity and a challenge to the partnership of sexuality and domination . . . We support the right of all people to live according to their sexual preferences without discrimination or fear of reprisals.

From Weather Underground. *Prairie Fire: The Politics of Revolutionary Anti-Imperialism*, 1974, pgs. 128-129

I wrote in my journal on July 31, 1974:

> Filled with chills, clouded with the beginning of tears, our chests heaving with joy and despair, the joy of reading the words of our life struggle, the despair of our toil and tears spread throughout the years of our history, the history of

our pain that has been conceived from the time of our birth. We need to realize our joyous despair and relish in the faith of our strength.

The benefits of being part of this movement of resistance, of major change, and, we hoped, of liberation undoubtedly outweighed the costs, but sometimes it astounds me how truly courageous we all were at the time. I did feel as though I had joined the revolution. My mother's confusion and embarrassment led her to wonder if I had joined a cult. I knew that I was part of a movement, even though sometimes I felt stranded on an alien planet where I was all alone. But I knew that I wasn't, especially during anti-rape collective meetings and women's dances, while combing the shelves of A Woman's Place Bookstore, and during those huge demonstrations, marches, and protests where I instantly felt a kind of transcendence that went far beyond myself.

Nothing would ever be the same.

LIGHTER THAN AIR

Yvonne Zipter

Three Mylar heart balloons pulse red
in the morning light, quivering
in a tree beside the freeway,
causing me to think
about my little family:
me, my wife, and the dog.
We are like different
appendages on the same
body. When we move,
we move together.
We carry our joy
like a long colorful canoe
to the shimmering lake
of our lives. Sorrow,
we can lift ten times
our weight of because
we are doing it together,
bending our legs before
we rise with it.
We tell each other lies
but only the best kind.
And though neither
my wife nor the dog
is in my sight as I write
these lines, like the Mylar
balloons, lost to my view
once I steered my way
onto the Touhy Avenue West
exit ramp, I can see them waving
(or, in the dog's case, wagging)

all friendly-like across eight
lanes of traffic, in my mind's
eye, which never blinks.

TRUE LOVE

Yvonne Zipter

Sometime in the night,
I rise to the top of my sleep
like weary cream & listen
to the rain, a train, & the painful snoring of my darling
wife. The very air
seems to trouble her.

I let the percussive
symphony play on a minute
or two, then move my hand
to cue the wind instrument
beside me to cease her solo.

But before my hand lands,
she has reached out
from her torpor to give it
a squeeze, then turns
over, banishing her stuttered
breathing for a time.

When I tell her in the morning
about the handclasp, she says:
You can't say I don't love you,
which I never do, even
when we have gotten ourselves
into a fervid boil of stupid
irritations, like milk about to form
an unpleasant temporary skin.

OLD FRIENDS

Olivia Swasey

"Do you still take it how you used to?" Janet asked, watching the hands across the table from her pour two little cartons of half-and-half into a chipped blue mug. The sugar packets went untouched.

"No. Realized the sugar was bad for my teeth. Just cream these days." Lou adjusted her watch, casting a subtle glance at the time, though not so subtle that Janet didn't notice.

"I'm sorry. If you have somewhere to be, that's all right; I won't keep you here." Janet folded her hands on the table next to her own coffee cup, picked at the nude nail polish on her thumb. She didn't look at Lou.

"I just don't wanna keep Gina waiting. I'm sure you understand."

"Yes."

A pause stretched out between them, the sounds of the diner filling in the space. At the next table, a waitress clinked glasses and cutlery together in a gray plastic bin balanced in one arm. The low thrum of afternoon conversation pervaded the air in the room; ceiling fans overhead spun in lazy circles.

#

When Lou had picked up the phone a week ago, the last voice she expected to find on the other end was Janet's.

"Hello?"

"Hey, Lou. Um, it's Janet." There was a long pause. The phone crackled static in the silence.

"Oh. Hey. It's been a while."

"Yeah . . . Listen, um, I'm going to be in town next Sunday, I'm—I'm passing through for work. Would you want to . . . get coffee with me? At the diner? You can come meet me after work, I'll be there in the evening. I just, ah. I just wanted to talk to you."

"Oh. Yeah, sure. That sounds nice. It'll be nice to . . . catch up."

"Right. Okay, then uh, next Sunday. Just come after work; I'll be waiting there. I'll see you soon."

"Okay, see you—" Lou started, but was cut off. She had hung up.

#

Janet had finished chipping the polish off her nail, so she looked up from her hands and met Lou's eyes. They gazed at each other for a moment; Lou was the first to look away. She sipped her coffee, set the mug down with a knock on the table and looked at her hands before cautiously raising her eyes to meet Janet's.

"Been with Gina now for a couple years. Do you . . . Did you meet anyone?"

"Oh," Janet looked down, laughed lightly, "no, um. No. I saw someone for a while, he . . . it's been a while. I'm not with anyone."

Lou made a sound of recognition in her throat and nodded.

"'S alright. Sometimes it's nice to be alone. Do your own thing. Figure yourself out." She took another sip of her coffee. Janet's had stopped steaming and was growing lukewarm in front of her.

"Of course." Janet looked out the window. The street was familiar. It had been a long time since she'd been here, had coffee.

"This used to be our place. Remember?" Janet said, still gazing out into the weedy parking lot.

"Yeah. We spent a lot of time here," Lou chuckled. "I remember, I met you while you were waiting on me. I started coming by damn near every day just to have a coffee and hope you were working."

"I know, I saw a lot of you then. I thought you were so handsome when you smiled. And you were a good tipper." Janet cracked a smile and looked at Lou, who grinned back. Suddenly, Lou dropped her smile and looked away, took another drink of her coffee, filtering the grounds through her teeth. Janet's face fell. They were quiet for a moment.

". . . How did you meet Gina?"

"Oh, we met at a bar. Nothin' special. Do you wanna see a picture of her?"

Janet nodded. "Mm-hmm," she said, leaning forward across the table as Lou pulled a thick wallet out of her back pocket. The brown leather was glossy from handling. Janet recognized it as the same one she'd given Lou for her thirtieth birthday. Ancient history now.

#

"Happy birthday, honey," Janet said, handing a small wrapped box to Lou before tucking her feet up underneath her on the couch. Lou smiled at her and began to tear away at the paper. "It's really nothing special, I just saw it and thought it would suit you." Lou opened the box to find a plain brown leather wallet.

"Oh, baby, I love it. Thank you," Lou said, leaning over to kiss Janet on the cheek. Janet ran a hand along the shirt seam at Lou's shoulder, her eyes soft.

"Only the best for you."

#

Lou flipped her wallet open to a photo insert. It was a photo of a woman in front of a car. She had a halo of curly, close-cropped red hair and a face full of freckles. She was smiling at the camera, nose and eyes crinkled as if caught in the middle of a laugh. Janet recognized the scenery—the photo had been taken at the drive-in movie theater at the edge of town. There was a Frisbee on the ground at the edge of the shot.

"She's beautiful. What does she do?"

"She's a grant writer. She has quite the way with words," Lou said, sliding her wallet back into her pocket.

"And you're still at the garage?"

"Yep. It's steady work, and I still like it. Don't see why that should change."

Janet nodded. Same old Lou.

#

"I hope you rot in this town forever, Louise!" Janet had screamed. There were tears running down her face. Neither of them said anything. Somewhere in the house, a clock ticked. Lou pressed her lips together, forming a thin line, then she nodded, scratched her hair a little.

"Right. I'm going to go for a walk." She shuffled her boots through the fragments of shattered china on the tile and walked out the side kitchen door into the night. As her footsteps receded, Janet's lip wobbled, and she covered her face with both hands, sinking into a crouch on the linoleum.

She was gone before Lou returned.

#

"What about you? You're in St. Louis last I heard, what are you doing there?"

"Oh, not much. I write for the *Riverfront Times* now. Still working on getting my stories into *The New Yorker*, you know me," Janet said with a smirk. Lou smiled.

"That's great Janet, I'm glad you're writing for a real paper now. You always deserved better than writing for our town's rinky-dink press." Janet's expression changed.

"They're a good publication, Lou. I loved the editorial team when I worked there," she said firmly, quietly. "Small and bad are not the same. You always . . ." Janet trailed off. Lou looked away. A waitress came by and refilled her coffee.

"Want me to refresh your cup honey?" she said. Janet looked up, distracted.

"Oh, no thank you, that's all right." The waitress shrugged and walked off. Janet sighed and looked at her coffee cup, still full but completely cold. They were quiet for a moment.

"Lou."

"Hmm?"

"I asked you here today because I needed to tell you something. I'm . . . I'm sorry." Janet tried to lift her eyes up to meet Lou's. They stared at each other. "I'm just sorry. For everything. I've been sorry every day for the last five years. I just needed you to hear it."

Lou nodded, her expression flat. She picked up her mug and drained the rest of her coffee.

"I'm going to go get some air," Lou said, moving to stand. She disappeared through the door of the diner, bells announcing her departure. Janet rubbed her face with both hands and heaved a sigh. Dropping a five on the table, she got up and went out the door, hoping Lou hadn't really left.

Lou was close to the diner, smoking a cigarette with a hand in her pocket. When Janet approached, Lou held out the pack wordlessly and Janet took one with a polite nod, lighting it with the offered matchbook. They stood silently smoking for a moment before Lou spoke.

"So. When do you think you'll be around again?"

Janet looked at the ground. "Not for a while. I was just in the area while I was travelling for work. I don't know when I'll be back." Lou nodded and ashed her cigarette.

"Well, I'll be here, just like always. You can call me anytime; you have my number. I'm glad you asked me to meet you."

"Thank you for agreeing to it. It was nice to see you again." Janet took a last drag from her cigarette before putting it out in the ashtray nearby. "I should be going. I'm trying to get back to St. Louis before it gets dark. You don't need a ride?"

"No, home is close enough, I can walk." There was a pause. Lou finished her cigarette. "It was good to see you, Janet." She reached out a hand and touched Janet's arm uncertainly, then let it drop.

"You too, Lou. Have a safe walk home," Janet said, lingering for a second longer before turning towards her car and walking away across the gravel parking lot. As she walked, there was a moment of silence before she heard Lou's footsteps begin to move away from the diner. Janet got in her car and turned out onto the street. As she drove along the road that would take her home, she glanced in the rearview mirror. In it, she could see Lou's broad-shouldered frame walking away. As the car moved, Lou receded further and further into the distance until finally, Janet couldn't see her anymore.

PENELOPE'S VISION
Natalie Eleanor Patterson

She knows it; seers recognize their visions
as distinct from other seeing.
—Cynthia Macdonald, "When Penelope Was Happy"

In another life, she marries in blue
a butch with matching vest, they dance
around the barn of their rustic reception after the ceremony
shakes the doves from their trees at forest-edge.
By now she's made new friends, doesn't recognize
the bridesmaids, but loves them all the same
as we love the strangers in our dreams.
Just like we love a bit of postwar irony:
the cake is red velvet, a massacre of sugar & cream
on her new spouse's face. They'll honeymoon
in Maine, adopt a mess of dogs, raise bees
not for their honey but for their lives.
She'll never sleep alone again, never wait
across a wine-dark sea. This she sees, somehow,
as she weaves.

LOVE POEM SANS PASSION

Natalie Eleanor Patterson

I wake up to the *touch of cinnamon* cereal, sliced apple,
windows open to mild February weather & stinkbugs
vaulting themselves   from the ceiling light. I shower
in fluorescence. I live the day as it crawls to me before the next
cold front sweeps through,   eating hard-boiled eggs,
Cloroxing doorknobs, swallowing vitamins.   I go
to bed. I wake up.   One day I walk the downtown bridge
over the dystopian ruins of Business 40 & a construction worker
waves to me from a truckbed   & I notify you
immediately.   I go to bed, wake up. It's cold again,
& I have bread & homework.   Overhead,
blackbirds congregate on telephone lines as I talk
myself to oblivion.   Here are the symptoms
of my week: Here are the emails I receive: Here
is my impossible task: I see you in every dust mote,
egg yolk, Chapstick, & paperweight,   let alone
the other stuff.   I find myself grateful, after all,
for futility.   I go to bed.   I wake up.
It is Tuesday.   I am in love.

BORDERS OF SALT
Fallen Kittie

Dana was born and raised in Wyandotte, but now she lives in K'jipuktuk. Her hometown was neither ever a home nor a town. It's a husk. Its ashen weeds are a vestige of the forest: plush in its past life, then razed to cultivate a county whose life is seasonal. Cabins are all that spring from the acreage. Lurid shingles and liners replace what vibrant pelts and plumage once roamed the land before. The city is the same except for a semblance of life that takes shape in wisps down the bar and the stray peal of smoke that curls from a chimney.

For Noor, it's in her voice; a voice that rolls over Dana like the plains whose stubble evinced a morsel of the green that once was. Noor reads a poem she spent the past week writing. Her chest swells to punctuate each note. Every so often, Noor's hand goes to her heart only to wander amidst stanzas. Dana watches as the fingers trail black and citrine kalamkaris which billow down her shoulders and around her skirt.

But it's her voice that grips Dana like a vice. Words fall from her in a warm, crisp timbre, words that are clearer than the streams that course to the ocean. Noor muses upon the city as a burrow that grows wider and darker the deeper she goes. She passes several bars on her way to work and several churches on her way to campus; but she says that, in the night, the blocks become indistinct.

So does Noor.

She turns red, pink, and blue in cosmic bursts of neon which showcase live girls or urge her to shoot pool. Some places have solicitors. They stalk after her even though she takes care to avoid their eyes. All the same, she says, desperate to make a patron out of a passerby. Piranhas starving for the lot. She peers skyward to find the sun, the clouds veiled by a grim palette of smog and concrete.

The writing circle is held every other morning, so it's perfect for Noor. She writes her best at sunrise. Her blood boils at night but cools in time to greet the horizon. Words burst from places she has yet to discern. Her heart hangs on her sleeve like her head. Her eyes are wild albeit perpetually downcast, alive but avoidant.

Many times, she turns up to the writing circle empty; but she inevitably shares. If she waits too long, the words hold her captive. She chafes like a spark, the precursor to the flame that arises when one strikes a match. The words hurtle within and claw their way out.

Noor speaks a lot with her hands. Today, they are adorned with henna which blends into lurid fractals across her palms. Dana thinks the scarlet ink betrays the proclivity of the flesh, the incandescence. Her hair does the same. It spills past her shoulders in glossy rivulets. They ripple to caress her cheeks, as if sex is woven into each strand. It is pungent like musk, bristled like pine.

Dana likes to write, but she starves for inspiration. In Noor, she has found a muse. It is Noor whom her poem embodies. Dana shares her latest: a tawny head of the valleys whose roots give rise to fruitful limbs and pasturage that tumbles into sage palates. The peak is marked by a russet garland with beads of malachite. There are dry vales which moisten beneath strokes. They swelter when she parts the glades. The fever breaks once they flourish.

When the circle applauds, Dana's eyes meet Noor's. An indecisive pulse hangs between them. It courses throughout the evening only to throb when the other women make themselves scarce.

The glossy cover of Dana's notebook contrasts the foolscap that creases within her grasp. Her mind drifts to a warm hereafter where she needs her hands to be free: one to caress the sex that crests her pubis, the other to flick the peaks of her breasts after she cups their expanse.

But Noor speaks in this moment: "I liked your reading. It was great."

Dana shrugs. "Not as great as yours."

"I guess quality is subjective."

Noor plants a kindred palm on Dana's shoulder, muses upon the threads of her cardigan. Her rouge fingers clash against the cold greys interlaced with periwinkle. She catches Dana tense, then release. It reminds her of the sleazy neon lights and discolored concrete; the relics of what once was now soured by rancid alleys, detached denizens, and boundless exhaust; and the scowl of headlights accompanying the cars that hiss past.

Noor imagines an evening of dark chaos. Peals of smoke and shadows would catch her breath, and the lips of another would catch her own. Obscured bodies in constant motion, like clockwork, switching like traffic lights, sirens, and horns that roll after engines, or the intermittent drags of a foreman's cigarette. The scent of jasmine pours from stalks of incense that singe in a tray on her windowsill. The bodies move over and over, faster and harder, to thrust a sex ingrained by fumes.

When Dana gives pause, Noor uncovers her phone. She volunteers her number and expects one in return.

#

Dana expects the hush over the line to end with a sharp click followed by a dial tone. As breaths pass by, she trembles when it doesn't. It means Noor is considering her offer.

It's too late to take it back.

"You're not far from me," Noor murmurs. "I can be there soon."

Noor arrives with a packet of incense and its wooden stand. She lights two stalks as Dana retrieves her notes. Noor's lips curl as she inhales. As Dana sits down on the couch, Noor reveals the scent is jasmine. It clears the air, she says. Dana finds that plausible as Noor sets about, redlining passages as she leafs through revisions.

She narrows her eyes. "Dana, this is good—but erratic."

Dana nods, resigned. "I've heard that before."

"So, you've heard it before, and you haven't listened?" Noor smirks. "Bad girl."

The incense begins to mist. Dana draws in the sweet smell. She softens with each breath. "I'm not a bad girl. I'm just a bad writer who does good every once in a while."

"When you write, what do you think about?"

"A woman."

"What woman?"

Dana chuckles. "She looks like you."

Noor starts to speak, but refrains. Whatever words she thought to muster hang behind her lips. Her eyes train upon Dana like a hawk, gauging every nuance she ponders to devour.

Everything is forgotten in one fell swoop.

Desire flares beneath Noor's fingertips which trace down Dana's cheek. They linger upon Dana's chest. When they pass Dana's collarbone to stop short of her breasts, Noor moves to bare her own. What follows is the rustle of Noor's shawls and skirts as they come undone to pool around her ankles.

Strands of dusk steal through the curtains as jasmine wafts from the windowsill. Dana wonders if she's dreaming. Noor hastens to close the space between them. The light casts a halo behind her.

Dana thinks of the valley. Breasts like mountains, crowned by pliant peaks; caverns foaming with thirst; and a rich hearth lying within the thicket of the sex.

Noor thinks of the city. Crooks and crevices fleshed by shingles or stone, and fissures that frame, then weep into orifices. Red lights pantomime legs, busts, and x's to divulge the cores held within asphalt.

No matter where you are, good things come to those who wait. Like the sexes which kiss. Not unlike the trees whose roots fork together, or the pavements whose every address is unicast, soldered in-line. There is a wall through every wood that forges its own path, caught in some way—any way—by resin. Likewise, there is a sylvan whose pulse beats within the metropolis in what grows through the concrete.

Noor guides Dana and several cushions off the couch, to the carpet. She undresses her, relishes the sex, lips pursed between her legs. As Dana stirs under her perusal, the mouth begins to weep. Pearls take shape and gather at the corners.

Noor leans in for a kiss. As she spreads the sex, the pearls cream against her lips and down her fingers. The folds glisten as her tongue pistons within. So do the curls that wreathe them.

The shadow of their bodies spills across the wall. Dana turns to it, clings to it as she struggles to prolong her pleasure. The shape takes no form. It runs like water, then heaves like a wave. Its length peaks as Noor climbs, pecking past her navel. She rises to Dana's breasts, cupping and suckling them like chalices. Her kisses ripple.

Dana urges Noor higher so that her tongue may undulate against hers. She strokes Noor's hair, then palms between them to ravel the fibrous thicket of her pubis. Her caress is curious, but incisive. She walks her fingers through every part of Noor. They survey the sex, bathe within until its musk grows rich, then tread to flick the posterior orifice.

In the distance, cries ring out from an assortment of beasts: horns which blare behind roaring engines, the rustle of leaves, sirens in pursuit, avian shrieks—except they're all drowned out. Noor and Dana are engrossed in the sounds of each other: the breaths, the suckles; the sounds of their fingers and tongues swimming, then crashing as they turn tidal. Sweat breaks the waves, but the intimates drench the nipples, mouths, and breasts.

Dana parts Noor's legs and solders her sex against hers, so that the lower mouths may kiss. She moves more intently now, harder and faster, desperate. Noor returns her thrusts, spurring to hasten the heat taking hold.

But the window is where Noor's pleasure swells. Dana kneels behind her. The curl of Dana's tongue throws shivers through her body. It seeks her core, flicks, and stills between the lips as Dana grasps her ass. Dana's face is buried between the mounds of flesh, licking, intent to burgeon the underbrush.

Dana thumbs the dimples at the base of Noor's spine, steering the hips to thrust so that the sex may yield its pleasure. The hearth calls from within.

Time slows to a crawl. Noor starts to tremble. Dana stands to offer Noor her mouth, ripe with musk to evince her delicious effort. Noor accepts. She purposes her every fiber into her mouth and hands to complement, to thrash, to mimic Dana's.

The women are driven by the waves building within them. They lock lips and limbs to come in unison. The climax hits them like an earthquake, and their toes curl as if the ground has split beneath their feet. As the jasmine hastens to ash, they drink in the view of a concrete tapestry and what shrubs emerge from the fissures.

DESCANT

Beth Brown Preston

One crystal morning we heard the song
of starlings awakened and perched on the wires.
The pale blue light slowly surrounded and aroused us.
Leaves of grass turned over and spilled their dew.
I remembered the past seven years
of emotion coursing between us
like a steady current of electricity.

Next to our bed a radio played the morning news.
Then Nancy Wilson sang:
"An older man is like an elegant wine"
as we resumed the odyssey of our true love.

The birds' song was a descant, an abstraction,
a work of jazz: a blues ode penned just for us two.

In one corner of the room my guitar slept
nestled in its black case waiting for my fingers' caress
when I took up my instrument
and reinvented the music.
Those same fingers of mine rustled
your silver hair and stroked your forehead.

I kept a journal of all the feelings and the music.
Today marked just one more epiphany
as we celebrated the birth of this morning's dawn.

SKETCH OF A FRONTIER WOMAN

Claudia Lars
(Translated by Beth Brown Preston)

Standing tall in the mire
unlike the flower's stalk
and the butterfly's eagerness . . .
without roots or fluttering:
more upright, more sure,
and more free.

Familiar with the shadow and the thorn.
With the miracle uplifted
in her triumphant arms.
With the barrier and the abyss
beneath her leap.

Absolute mistress of her flesh
to make it the core of her spirit:
vessel of the heavenly,
domus aurea,
a lump of earth from which rise, budding,
corn and tuberose.

Forgotten the Gioconda smile.
Broken the spell of centuries.
Conqueror of fears.
Clear and naked in the limpid day.

Lover without equal
in a love so lofty
that today no one divines it.
Sweet,

with a filtered sweetness
that neither harms
nor intoxicates him who tastes it.

Maternal always,
without the touch that hinders flight,
or the tenderness that confines,
or the petty yieldings that must be redeemed.

Pioneer of the clouds.
Guide to the labyrinth.
Weaver of tissues and songs.
Adorned only in simplicity.
She rises from the dust . . .
unlike the flower's stalk
which is less than beauty.

GOD SO WILLS

Gabriela Mistral
(Translated by Beth Brown Preston)

The very earth will disown you
If your soul barters my soul;
In angry tribulation
The waters will tremble and rise.
My world became more beautiful
The day you took me to you.
When under a flowering thorn tree
Together we stood without words,
And love pierced us with the heavy
Fragrance of its thorn.

The earth will vomit forth snakes
If ever you barter my soul!
Barren of your child, and empty,
I rock on my desolate knees.
Christ in my breast will be crushed,
And the charitable door of my house
Will break the wrist of the beggar,
And repulse the sorrowful woman.

The kiss your mouth gives another
Will echo within my ear,
As the deep surrounding caverns
Bring back your words to me.
Even the dust of the highway
Guards the scent of your footprints.
I track them, and like a deer
Follow you into the mountains.

Clouds will paint over my dwelling
The image of your new love.

Go to her like a thief, crawling
In the guts of the earth to kiss her.
When you lift her face you will find
My face disfigured with weeping.

God will not give you light
Unless you walk by my side.
God will not let you drink
If I do not tremble in the water.
He will not let you sleep
Except in the hollow of my hair.

If you go, you destroy my soul
As you trample the weeds by the roadside.
Hunger and thirst will gnaw you,
Crossing the heights of the plains;
And wherever you are, you will watch
The evening skies bleed with my wounds.
When you call another woman
I will issue forth on your tongue,
Even as the taste of salt
Deep in the roots of your throat.
In hating, or singing, in yearning
It is me alone you summon.

If you go and die far from me
Ten years your hand will be waiting
Hollowed under the earth
To gather the drip of my tears.
And you will feel the trembling
Of your corrupt flesh,
Until my bones are powdered
Into dust on your face.

WILD NIGHTS — LESBIAN LIVES! THE EMILY DICKINSON HOMESTEAD, REVISITED

Jessica Lowell Mason

What level of Sapphic madness, or divinest sense, does one have to acquire to have one's house turned into a museum after one's death?

This tenderly morbid question came to my lesbian writer's mind while carrying in the mail to my homestead in East Amherst, New York on a drab Friday afternoon during an extended winter that had determined to stretch its abominable bluster into the month of May, delaying the flowers, making them especially long awaited.

I had received a letter from a lesbian. A closeted lesbian. One of my closest friends. Examining the way her ink bled in a shoddy, haphazard, yet still professorial job of jotting down the respective addresses of our lesbian homesteads, I ripped through the back of the envelope. Upon entry into my house, while mid-sentence in conversation with one of my housemates, I tugged two fingers into the valley of the envelope and pulled out a small yellow note folded around a questionnaire. Barely paying attention and about to set it down, two words caught my eye: Emily Dickinson. I pinched it one moment longer, long enough to steal an entire sentence. My friend wrote that she thought Emily Dickinson would be appalled by the idea that her domicile has been turned into a museum.

I set down the note and went swiftly to the dining room to set down my books and fell into an upholstered chair in the living room. Thoughts unfurled in my mind, thoughts about lesbians and letters and names and houses. My thoughts transported me to my freshman year at Hampshire College, where I spent a good deal of time in the well-windowed classrooms and on the benches of Emily Dickinson Hall.

Emily Dickinson Hall housed a theatre, appropriately, and it was encountering this Main Stage Theatre daily that allowed me to weigh, back and forth, whether I would have the courage to audition for a show. I thought I should like to be in the Sapphic production of Stein's *Tender Buttons*, and so I bought a collection of her work at a local bookstore, but my still-seventeen brain was not ready to comprehend what it later came to understand. I was the Girl of Emily Dickinson Hall that first semester. I frequently found myself alone in the hall; it was somewhat of a sanctuary to me, scared as I was of life and conflicted as I was by my self-chosen isolation, preferring the company of a ghost. Alone in this hall, I greeted passersby, strangers and familiars alike, and I was as active as one could be—in my mind and with my pen. I longed. To be exactly where I was but to be there with someone. Someone I loved. That someone was the ghost of Emily Dickinson Hall, my desired companion, my distant devoted, the two of us, girl and ghost, the beasts and bell(e)s of Amherst who knew exactly for whom we would address our letters, fold our pages, enclose our words, roar, toll. There was something about a hall named after a woman who lived an unconventional, Sapphic life on her own terms that made me feel at home. I was a girl navigating my own early Sapphic life the symbolic hall where all of my Luna bars were consumed. I was dwelling in possibility until I grew too impatient to dwell in that hall, without answers, any longer. Those were some of the most romantic days of my life, and I spent them alone in the hall of a Sapphic ghost.

The next Dickinsonian flight of fancy took hold of me, and I thought about my closeted friend's suspicion about Emily Dickinson's post-mortem appraisal of what had become of her writings and her homestead. I could not help but battle it out, imagining somehow that Emily would be able to understand why a lesbian like me should want to lie awake and dream on all the benches in her hall, should burst with tearful ecstasy standing by her bed, looking out her window, beholding her pen. *But what about her homestead? And what about mine?*

Then I entered into a maze of ideas about writers and their houses: how the house comes to emblemize writers, how the writer might be subsumed or exhumed, revered and worshiped or exploited through the structure of the house. *But what is the relationship between a lesbian and her homestead, I wondered, still. And what is home? Is it our halls? Our letters? Our erased names? Our ghosts?*

I have lived in a number of houses, but were I a lesbian writer of Dickinson's magnitude, which one should be made into a museum? This one, of course. My father's estate, the one in which I resided long ago and now once again reside. My museum could only be here, in this house where I grew to love a woman, where I first read Emily Dickinson's poems by candlelight in my bedroom, where I shared bits and pieces of Dickinson with my ceilings and with my beloved who read Dickinson's poetry, too. *This home, this room: this would be my museum. But what would they get right? And what would they erase? What would they misrepresent during the curation? Would they say I danced in front of my window every night in high school as a symbolic gesture because the window of the woman I loved was directly across from mine? Would they say something of my mad ideas about the language of the blinds?*

Could this house now belonging to my father be someday named after me? The Jessica Lowell Mason Homestead. The idea forced laughter, sarcasm, delight. *Could the fire of my spirit overcome his patriarchal inheritance?* By the time these thoughts flooded my mind, I was skipping across the driveway, past the mailbox out onto Chasewood Lane, taking a photograph of my homestead, noting the upper room, the madwoman's room in the left corner, determined to haunt it forever. Imagine: a homestead belonging to a lesbian. Imagine: people caring about her legacy, not caring if she were mad or not, understanding that madness is always a construct of a particular time and that the mad are often those pushing into the future.

I took my photo and flung myself back toward the homestead, thinking thoughts made of mutters about shutters: *I'm okay with this house being made into a museum as long as the shutters are painted to their former shade of red instead of this terrible shade of blue that my father allowed. What if the ice storms further damage my favorite tree? What if the next owners of this house remove the tree because they have no sense, no taste, no devotion to greenery? Will there be a memory of a tree . . . or will that be erased from the homestead, like Emily's lesbianism?*

Long after we are gone and our memories have been manipulated and erased, our homesteads will remain, and the windows, too. If our stories are never told, the windows into our minds and hearts never opened, if our very essences are erased from our homesteads, the structures will revolt, in their way, and we will be the ghosts in the halls haunted by girls who are determined to know us, respect us, learn from us, continue our struggles and work.

I entered my house, turned off the camera, and opened the letter from my friend. Wrapped inside her note was an interview with Molly Shannon about a film I knew nothing about: *Wild Nights with Emily*. Hours later, I walked out of the local theater having giggled, choked up, cursed, grunted, and sighed throughout the entire film. My wild night well spent. I watched it and felt a deep intimacy with the film. I understood its humor; I understood the pain beneath it. Most of all, I understood that, finally—finally—someone had understood so many of the frustrations and motivations, barriers and exultations, that have influenced and been at work in me. I make no claims about any kind of universal lesbian experience; lesbianism is experienced uniquely by anyone who claims the identity. But I do feel connected with Emily Dickinson, and I have since I first read her poems during my youth. I know what it is to taste in every part of my mind and spirit "a liquor never brewed."

I also know what it is to walk down the path between the houses of Emily and Susan at The Emily Dickinson Homestead. Last summer, I walked the path with my friend and a kitten who accompanied our group. The closeness between Emily and Susan was alluded to, gently remarked upon, but extraordinarily understated during the tour. Surely, *Wild Nights with Emily* will shake all of Amherst. Surely the ghosts of the homesteads will be brought to life again and renewed.

Why do we commit the longings of our souls onto paper? Why do we fold our hearts and send them across the footpath in the hands of the ones who haven't yet learned to read souls?

Lesbians and letters have long been entangled, dating back to Sappho's fragments. Those that have been recovered, at least. So many of our poems and letters have been torn, tossed, crumpled, shredded, or burned. So much of our love has been prevented, thwarted, given the ax of patriarchal expectation, that maintaining intimate relations has come to mean reading and writing in the halls of ghosts. So much of our lives are spent recovering: our pasts, the fragments of our hystories, our beloveds, ourselves. Being enmeshed in the trope and real struggle of recovery is often part and parcel of the experience of being a lesbian or of living and loving on the Sapphic continuum. And at the heart of this recovery is the homestead. Not the curated one. Not the museum with the gift shop. The letters in our hearts, the desires in our minds, the inner parts of us that we begin nurturing at birth—all that we nurture, all that springs from the pen.

My home is in the ink we share and shed.

VARIATIONS ON A MINOR THIRD

Samira Negrouche
(Translated by Marilyn Hacker)

For Angélique Ionatos

>   You seeking truth
>   It's the wall you're seeking
>   One stone another stone another.
>   Lean your back against the wall
>   or your forehead
>   and stand like that all night long
>   with the little coins in your pockets
>   that make no gold
>   or silver sound
>   are worth nothing.
>   Like dreams.
>
>   *Yannis Ritsos*
>   *Papers*

One

Maddened waves break and unfurl
bodies unfeathered   washed away
unbearable corrida of blood-red voice

go and go and come
in oscillating rhythm
of the aquatic   neck
seismic pulse-beat

**

Phantom silhouette drifts
across footsteps of memory
that slip away   vanish

an undulating wire beckons
the closer you come
the more it eludes you in the current
of an obsessive repetitive dream
you move forward your steps
volatile   noiseless
on the arrhythmic path   your steps
impotent   breathless
the wire passes
and does not wait

**

In the hollow of a blind spot
the instant of a sixteenth-note
uncertainly struck
twinned bellies at low tide
breath held
waiting

**

Uncoiling
of sea stars
goddesses' nuptials of O
Olympia of aural velvet
opened to these fingers
roots
that grasp the sky
To cover you
and draw you out
on a note with wings.

Two

Not to lose you
in the desert of waves

Frightened women
on a deafened shore
the sea is a refrain
Temperamental
those children
who wait out seconds
like hours

**

Poseidon's messenger
as you glide above the shifting
sands of your infinite jungle
free this mirage-filled horizon
your maddened mountains
and your spellbinding honey
open this heaven of mysteries
and carry the avid
headlong plea
draw your angry wave
across the wire of waiting
the shore is an orphan.

**

So near its tongue
the voice is mute

**

You are a small boat growing distant
in tomorrow's dawn

so spread your wings and wipe me dry
with an innocent smile
that will slip away silent

**

I wait only for the return
of a shapeless echo
that draws the deletions
of a story with weight
but no measure

**

Maritime drift
of my centenary nights
your lover's uncovered her breasts
and returns you to other drownings

**

Not to take you
reined-in desire of an image
that shatters on solid ground

Three

The hand's embrace
trembling and tectonic
parade of dervish waves
tamed horizon
of these unacknowledged dreams

**

Small woman
behind the frenzied honking

the day of a championship match
pale on a hill in Algiers
abandoned and afraid
men's emptiness, madness
in the besieged theater

**

A syllable's
high-voltage magic
known, recognized language
as the jugular bulges
defines itself
and invades the epidermal space

**

Centenary embrace
or why not bi-millennial
of an uprooted orange

**

Men who cry victory
who breathe in the hip
of a red and black ball
this is a circle stripped
of its fraternal islets

**

Spellbinding, she sings
a sister bejewels her
amnesiac earth

**

Murmur that lives in me
there on the dusty cord

I am offered to unknown labile
migratory birds

**

The percussion is a divine
submission
does not know that return is departure

LETTERS

May 2019
Dear Julie,

112 just arrived in my mailbox yesterday. I looked at it, smiled, and breathed a sigh of relief for you. Hope you can kick back and relax for a bit. Job well done.

I sat down in my reading chair and read the first half, took a yogurt and fruit break and finished the second half.

Enjoyed your piece on Michelle Cliff. I didn't know much about her, so it was an eye opening read for me.

My favorite poem was Lavender Black by Yeva Johnson. Like it very much.

Emel Karakozak's work is exquisite. She is the daughter Tee Corinne never had. I was amazed by her work. I do wish the quality of the printing had been better though. Was that the glitch at the printer you mentioned?

Now . . . I did happen to notice that Madrone was on fire. Fortunately she still has a platform where she is still able to express her fire. It was good to see you didn't take it personally.

You handled your response to her very well. I am always aware that you speak from your heart, as well as your experience. There is no doubt in my mind that you always have the best interest of Sinister Wisdom at heart, and that is the job, at least the volunteer job.

To be honest, my opinion lies somewhere between yours and hers. Definitely closer to yours, but that is the beauty of Sinister Wisdom. We all still have a place for our Lesbian voices.

I am glad to know that you are going to be around for some time to come You can always count on my support, Julie.

In sisterhood,
Jill [Crawford]

[In an email]

To everyone involved—massive kudos and Bravissimas for a job clearly lovingly done, and also done superlatively, extremely, amazingly and excitingly WELL DONE!!

It's a GREAT work, way above even some of the better 'blank books with quotes' I've seen and own.

Two are quite actively journals for me already, one is already wrapped as a gift for my beloved niece.

Thank you for your persistence with SW too. Your calling is our great good fortune.

Lotsa love,
ReaRae I. Sears

An Open Letter to Julie R. Enszer: Who Does Inclusion Exclude?

I am writing about a response to a letter in Sinister Wisdom #112, Spring 2019. In response to Hawk Madrone's thoughtful letter about the loss of lesbian space in SW, you said, "Nothing in SW [in the] past eight years of publishing . . . erases lesbians or lesbian space."

I take serious offense to your assertion and want to share my reasons why. I will be sending this letter to Lesbian Connection and SW both in the hopes it will be published and open the discussion further. I will also be publishing it online. First, I would like to explain my language choices. In order for this to be palatable to the widest range of lesbian readers, I am going to avoid using pronouns in reference to transwomen and use neutral language (for example, using the gender-inclusive term of "male people" instead of "men" for people who were born male.) These concessions of language are my peace offering to my lesbian sisters who will fiercely disagree with this letter.

For some personal background, I am a lesbian woman who was groomed into queer ideology and subsequently sexually abused by a much older trans woman, when I was a lesbian teenager. I spent several years lost in a "queer" identity in a few different physically, sexually & emotionally abusive relationships with trans women. I was able to escape from my longest abusive relationship with my life and was able to find my way back to my lesbian reality with the help of many wonderful women.

Part of my experience of coming home as a lesbian has been exploring lesbian herstory, including a hunger for the many viewpoints presented in lesbian periodicals. My girlfriend and I buy up (and borrow!) all the copies of SW, Lesbian Ethics, and Common Lives/Lesbian Lives we can. One such issue we managed to get our hands on was Sinister Wisdom #95 from Winter 2015.

I was aware that after Sinister Wisdom changed editors in 2014,[1]* the publication expanded to allow submissions from male people who claim a lesbian identity. I was prepared for that. What I wasn't prepared for was finding an article submission by a trans woman named Michelle Lynne Kosilek.

The article is titled Mutagenic Diaspora. In it, an incarcerated trans woman uses the term disapora, which I have only ever heard used by people separated from their indigenous lands, to describe the feeling of gender dysphoria. Kosilek refers to having a "little girls' heart," says "natal females have mostly been freed from the patriarchal slavery where a woman's value was inextricably linked to her willingness to be subservient and bear children," celebrates a ruling in favor of receiving vaginoplasty, and talks about the plight of trans women who identify as lesbians in prison.

Kosilek finishes the article with: "As women, as lesbians, as feminists, we are stronger and more deserving than that." The sentence is part of an argument about gaining free access

---

1 * Julie R. Enszer became the editor of *Sinister Wisdom* with Merry Gangemi in 2010.

to state-funded women's attire, makeup, uterine transplants, vaginoplasties, and housing in a women's prison. But my letter is not to argue the merits of sex-segregated spaces or state-funded transition.

Let me tell you why Michelle Kosilek is in prison. In May 1990, Kosilek's wife Cheryl McCaul came home and found Kosilek wearing her clothes. She was upset. According to Kosilek, she threw a cup of tea. We'll never know if that even happened. What we do know is that Kosilek first strangled Cheryl with a rope, then with piano wire, nearly decapitating her from the force used. Kosilek drove her body to a local mall and dumped her there. Her body was found with her top pulled up and her pants pulled down. Kosilek claims to have no memory of the murder and that it was in "self-defense" due to the trauma of Cheryl's negative reaction to finding her husband wearing her clothes and allegedly being doused with a hot cup of tea.

This is what the court record states: "With regard to deliberate premeditation, the evidence would permit a rational jury to infer that the defendant waited until the victim's son was at work, that he approached his wife from behind with a wire, and strangled her by tightening the wire around her neck. With regard to extreme atrocity or cruelty, the prosecution's expert testified that: there were multiple wounds on the victim's body; she was strangled by a wire and then a rope; she was conscious for at least fifteen seconds after strangulation began and remained alive for three to five minutes; and there were indications of a conscious struggle."

A male person killing a female partner—we, as lesbians with feminist consciousness, know the this is part of a pattern: male violence. We know this happens often. One estimate I've heard is three women a day. I see these stories every day—locally, nationally, globally. Those of us who have experienced male violence as little girls and/or grown women know it goes on and on and on.

I should not have had to read the manifesto of a male person who carried out a lethal, brutal act of male violence in the pages of a lesbian feminist publication. I did not seek out this experience. I was not scouring issues for something to upset me as a survivor of male violence perpetrated by trans women. I simply started reading an issue I had felt I was lucky to obtain and was retraumatized by the casual inclusion of a "lesbian & feminist" manifesto from a male person who held piano wire taut around a woman's neck and watched her as she struggled & died.

I read this article in February 2018. I have hardly picked up an issue of Sinister Wisdom since. I have kept my silence about this article but find myself willing to do so no longer. The idea that we can have lesbian space, especially lesbian separatist space, that includes male people is not a neutral idea. This is not a win-win situation. Where there are male people, there is male violence. This is not to say that lesbians cannot abuse and harm each other greatly. That reality is not up for debate. But this is not that, and it never will be.

To say the inclusion of this male murderer does not erase lesbians or negate the intention of lesbian space is ludicrous. It is insulting to all lesbians. It is especially insulting to lesbians who have faced male violence or sexual & emotional misconduct from male people who identify as lesbians while trying to navigate lesbians spaces which are more and more "inclusive" of trans women identifying as lesbians and more and more hostile towards lesbians who do not include male people in their sexuality or wish to gather or organize with them.

To try to fence-sit on this issue is in some ways admirable and certainly understandable. I know many lesbians trapped in this balancing act. But for some of us, the fence ran out and we found we had our backs against a wall. There is no "inclusion" of transwomen without the heavy cost of excluding lesbians like me. My story is not unique. Upon coming out, many lesbians of my generation have been targeted by transwomen for this type of abuse. Please do not "include" male people in lesbian culture, when that makes it untenable for some of us to participate anymore. I hope you will reconsider your decision to "include" this perpetrator in SW, and understand you made that decision at the expense of lesbian survivors.

I am no longer willing to stay silent on this issue, so I am choosing to speak out.

Thank you for your time.

Kitty Robinson

Statement from the *Sinister Wisdom* Board of Directors

For many years, *Sinister Wisdom* has opened the doors wide to include transgender and gender non-conforming lesbians, bisexuals, and queers across the gender spectrum, and we will continue to have open doors for all lesbians: non-binary lesbians, trans women lesbians, trans men lesbians, agender lesbians, lesbian feminists, lesbian feminist separatists, and woman-identified-woman lesbians, to name but a few. Who we are and how we identify will vary greatly, and open arms will not keep us safe from harm, but we believe that a policy of openness and curiosity about all lesbian lives sparks creative work, opens community dialogue, and instills in us, as lesbians, a free-thinking people, excitement for a place to further our work, support each other, challenge ourselves, and sometimes disagree with work within these pages and editions of *Sinister Wisdom*. We trust our readers to enjoy and be inspired by lesbian writing, and know that sometimes writing may disturb or cause disagreements. In fact, this is paramount. We struggle with this, too, and make our struggles visible.

The crime of murder that Michelle Kosilek committed disturbs us. We do not all agree about publishing the piece. Even so, we want to hold space for many ideas, including subscriber critique, while supporting editorial autonomy. *Sinister Wisdom* is and always has been dedicated to print work that is difficult, provocative, uncomfortable, and radical across many nuances of the word. This is how we learn and grow, and it means we include voices that may provoke a variety of feelings and discussions.

We continue to publish these complexities and welcome the discussions that follow that are supportive or critical in productive ways. We anchor space for new ideas and support the practice of editorial independence. We stand behind how our editors expand *Sinister Wisdom's* dedication to the inclusion of women in prison. However we look at it together, we have conflicted feelings. And, we support each other. We struggle even among ourselves except in this: we are all lesbians in support of incarcerated women including trans women of color and sex workers; an important part of our mission is to be accessible to incarcerated women, and this means women who commit crimes. Our kind of compass includes radical inclusivity. The emotional capacity to sit with newness, a multi-faceted way of being human in the world, is difficult. There is an ongoing need for new questions and new answers. We are a woven fabric of experience. Within this fabric, we make our struggles visible.

    Sinister Wisdom Board of Directors, June 2019
    Roberta Arnold
    Tara Shea Burke
    Cheryl Clarke
    Julie R. Enszer
    Sara Gregory
    JP Howard
    Joan Nestle
    Rose Norman
    Red Washburn

INTERVIEWS WITH MERRIL MUSHROOM ABOUT HER PLAY *BAR DYKES*

Rose Norman

As part of New York City's celebration of the fiftieth anniversary of Stonewall, the city's oldest LGBTQ professional theatre group, TOSOS (The Other Side of Silence), produced Merril Mushroom's one-act play about Miami Beach and New York City lesbian bars in the 1950s, *Bar Dykes*. The TOSOS audience sat around the sides of a set consisting of a small bar with cash register, three tables, and a juke box, all props for various courtship rituals and other small dramas over an evening of dykes looking for love. The show ran off-off Broadway for four long weekends (Thursday–Saturday) at The Flea, a 50-seat theatre in lower Manhattan, and was well reviewed.[2] Merril Mushroom has been a subscriber and contributor to *Sinister Wisdom* since its very first issue in 1976. Although she does not consider herself a playwright, and wrote the play in the 1980s as a lark for playing with already-outdated stereotypes, the TOSOS production brings new light to how far we have come since the days when only "butches" could court "femmes," unless you were "ki-ki" (rhymes with mai tai) and swung both ways.

Rose Norman interviewed Merril Mushroom by phone before the play opened and several times during its run.[3]

Q: What gave you the idea to write about the butch-femme dynamic in dyke bars?

I had written a narrative piece called "How to Engage in Courting Rituals 1950s Butch-Style in the Bar," all about the

---

2 Reviews are linked at www.merrilmushroomsbardykes.com.

3 TOSOS posted the one-hour July 1 interview recording online at https://chirb.it/E4a61h?fbclid=IwAR2jb9odBZ-g2phUPbrl4C-2evDSziYNLeGdJ68QRDyffuLc7S6oarTvTbQ.

different ways that butches courted femmes at that time. I was writing for a lot of lesbian and gay magazines in order to get free copies [they usually paid only in free copies], and courting rituals came up because my friends and I would often spoof the different ways we would behave back in the day—the way you would sit, the way you would hold your cigarette, the ways you would come on to somebody. It was a popular article and was reprinted several other places after *Common Lives/Lesbian Lives* published it.[1] We mimed "Courting Rituals" several times at Womonwrites. Somebody would play the part of the butch, and somebody would play the part of the femme, and somebody would play the part of the bartender, while someone else read the lines.

We kind of parodied ourselves back then because we were an oppressed minority and lived a life of being in danger all of the time, always under some kind of a threat. Making fun of ourselves *for ourselves* was okay. It's really more of a parody than the way things actually happened. Subtly they happened that way. You know when you flick your cigarette pack and the cigarettes rise up just those particular three measurements, the butches did do that, and it took a lot of practice. It was kind of a showy thing like fancy dancing and *posing* at the juke box. It wasn't that that kind of behavior was going on at all times and was predominant in the bar itself. If you looked, you could see it was going on, and the play exaggerates it.

Q: Were any of the characters based on particular people you knew? Did you identify with any of the characters?

---

[1] First published in no. 4 (summer 1982): 6-10. See also "Bar Dykes Sketches: 1959," *Common Lives/Lesbian Lives*, no. 5 (fall 1982): 17-22. "Courting Rituals" was reprinted in *Mae West Is Dead: Recent Lesbian and Gay Fiction* (1983), *The Penguin Book of Lesbian Short Stories* (1994), and several places online. Quotations from the play were used to caption fashion pictures in the magazine *10 Percent* (March/April 1995).

Every one of them, but composites. All of the dialogue is actual words that I had heard said at different times. The whole thing about "My Mother Just Found Out I'm Gay," the breakups, the cruising. Every bit of the dialogue is accurate. But I didn't see myself in them. Now I did do some of the posturing—I was good at that Zippo lighter, running it up my jeans to get it to light!

Q: One of the characters is described in stage directions as a "drag butch," a term we don't use these days. What does that mean? And how do you define "butch" and "femme"? Is it role-playing or something more?

A drag butch is a woman who dresses in men's clothing, and often passes as a man. She sometimes binds her breasts with an Ace bandage. It was role play to a degree, but also really, really serious. The only role models we had for coupleness were male and female, so we had that duality—not everywhere, but in the bar scene there was more delineation between butch and femme. People would say, well the butch is the man and the femme is the woman, but that's not really how it was. Or people would say the butch is the dominant and the femme is the passive, but that's not how it was either. In the role play, it played out like that, but there's an inherent sense of being deep inside that they can relate as either butch or femme, and they usually overlap a little. The best way I could describe it is that butch is that which is not femme, and femme is that which is not butch.

It was a really, really big deal that butches did not go with butches, and femmes did not go with femmes. Every once in a while a femme would go with a femme, but nobody took them seriously. I knew several women who were "stone butches" (untouchable butches), who were in love with each other, but neither one would bend. I remember a time when my friend Julia Penelope (who was butch) in all innocence went to bed with another butch, and later at the beach someone said to her, very derisively, "Oh, I hear you went femme for (whoever it was)," and the derision was so intense that it was years later before Julia let anybody touch her again.

Q: It's hard to talk about the butch/femme scene in your play without thinking of the current trend toward transitioning if you are leaning toward one gender or another. Is what we now call "gender identity" at play in these butch-femme roles?

I guess you could call [the butch/femme roles] gender identities since they have to do with gender. Gender identity is a broad topic. Some people think they are a man trapped in a woman's body, or a woman trapped in a man's body. I can understand that. I can think of a couple of stone butches back then who today might be considered transgender. I knew several women in Miami who routinely passed as men, and one woman who came to Miami from New York who was taking black market testosterone she had bought on the street (it wasn't available otherwise).

But most butches, even the drag butches, weren't trying to be men. We were trying to "pass" as men. We didn't really like men all that much, and we certainly didn't want to be a man, but we would *love* to have all the goodies that men got just by being men—like a better paying job, or the ability to walk down the street holding the hand of the woman we loved, or a little more respect in public places, or not being name-called or put in jail or in mental hospitals. We saw the great place that men had in the world, and we wanted a piece of it.

Q: How did class enter into the butch/femme scene?

Sometimes butches couldn't get as good jobs as femmes could, so they might wind up driving a tram or working in a restaurant kitchen. If they were educated, they could get white-collar jobs, but they had to be really careful not to be outed. Femmes had to be careful, too. Many femmes were sex workers, some entertainers, some waitresses, some nurses, teachers—all the female professions. They could get by with more in the white-collar world, because they could pass more easily. Femmes have gotten a lot of flak over the years from feminists and other lesbians who blame them for being able to pass. We weren't blaming so much back then. Our survival was different. We didn't have the luxury of blaming each other for trying to survive. We had to watch out for the law, and if somebody could pass, sometimes we'd get them to front for us to do something we couldn't otherwise get away with.

Q: I expect that Miami in the 50s was very racially segregated, yet you chose to make one of your characters, Linda, Black. The TOSOS production also casts two other characters as women of color. Racism doesn't enter into the discourse of the play. Is this anachronistic?

Yes and no. Every once in a while a Black dyke (usually a call girl or hooker) would show up at a bar, but in general we were pretty segregated. The Black gay kids, mainly men, went to the two bars in Liberty City or Overtown, the Black sections of Miami. I don't remember anything at all about any Black lesbians there. There was more mixing at the bars in New York City (where I moved in the 1960s), but not even that much. In Florida and New York both there was a lot of class segregation. Actually, Linda is patterned after a particular Black dyke I knew from New York. She was the only Black character I had written into the play, to show the scarcity. In the '50s, we were just becoming conscious of these issues as things that we could actually change, should change. Sexism took even longer to come to consciousness! I really like it with more diversity the way TOSOS cast it.

Q: What inspired the 2019 TOSOS production of *Bar Dykes*?

I wrote the play back in the 1980s, but after my house burned down in 2015, everything I owned burned up. So people were sending me copies of my writings, and someone sent me a copy of the *Bar Dykes* manuscript. I showed it to my friend

Faythe Levine, who is an artist and art curator. She showed it to a friend in Brooklyn, Caroline Paquita, and they collaborated on publishing the manuscript in 2016. I sent a copy of that to my friend Bob Patrick, an accomplished playwright who had lived across the hall from me in New York, but who now lives in California. In the 1980s, he had produced it in Los Angeles, and also in Florida. He sent a copy of the republished script to Kathleen Warnock, back in New York. Kathleen is associate artistic director of TOSOS.[2] Through TOSOS, she organized a reading at the Queerly Festival at the Kraine Theater in New York in June 2018, and then TOSOS produced it in summer 2019.

Q: The TOSOS board of directors struggled with the word "dykes" in your title, thinking it would be viewed as a slur. What did you call yourselves back then? Lesbians? Bar dykes? Gay? Was gay in common usage?

Gay was the ONLY word we used. We were gay girls at gay bars at a gay beach, going to gay parties; and we often spoke of the irony in using that word when gay life was often so tragic. I looked up the common usage and derivation and found that common usage goes back to the 1930s, derivation back a couple of centuries.

Over a thousand actors responded to TOSOS's *Bar Dykes* cast call for eleven female roles, posted on Actors Access, more submissions than TOSOS had ever received. Their production of *Bar Dykes* ran for twelve performances, almost always to sold out houses, and the ensemble cast became close and very engaged through the show. It got positive reviews in *Curve* and *ArtForum* as well as reviews and notices in over a dozen other media outlets. In depicting the extremes of butch/femme role-playing in the 1950s,

---

2 See Kathleen Warnock's "Butches and Femmes After Dark in the '50s," June 18, 2018, GayCityNews.com - https://www.gaycitynews.nyc/stories/2018/13/w30649-butches-femmes-dark-50s-2018-06-18.html

during twenty-first century conflict over non-binary and transgender identities, the play is meaningful and timely—and funny. For information about ordering the script or producing the play, go to www.merrilmushroomsbardykes.com.

BOOK REVIEWS

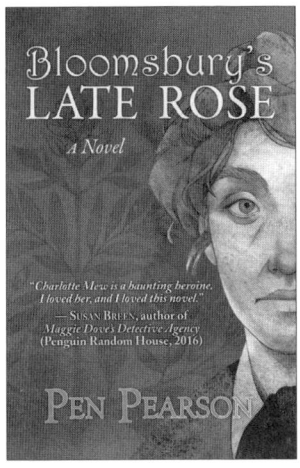

Bloomsbury's Late Rose
by **Pen Pearson**
Chickadee Prince Books, 2019
Paperback 266 pages, $14.99

Reviewed by Samantha Pious

Pen Pearson's historical novel *Bloomsbury's Late Rose* traces the life of turn-of-the-twentieth-century poet Charlotte Mew as deftly as we might imagine Mew herself sketching out the measures of her best-known poem, "The Farmer's Bride"—in pastels or charcoal, with a pianist's delicate hand. In the childhood Pearson imagines for her, Charlotte does play piano, but it is her sister Anne, the painter, whom she sees as a true artist.

After their siblings Henry and Freda are both institutionalized with a mental illness which seems to be hereditary, Anne and Charlotte, in their early twenties, vow never to marry so as never to pass on the "family curse." For Anne, courted by the handsome Mr. Anthony, this resolution proves difficult to keep. But Charlotte has her own reasons for choosing to remain unmarried. When the witty, dashing novelist May Sinclair walks into her life, will Charlotte still hold to the sisters' pact? Or will she follow her desire for the love of another woman? And what of her dreams and her sister's, their shared longing for recognition and posterity as artist and poet?

Imagining what experiences might have inspired Mew's best poems, Pearson opens a window into the author's psyche, performing a labor of love that is at once speculative and essential. Of "Requiescat" (composed, according to this novel's chronology, in 1909), Pearson writes:

> There it was again, the melodic and insistent voice of Middle C, bobbing on the distant waves of time. [. . .] First, in descriptive phrases, she sketched images of Nunhead and the countryside of the Isle of Wight. The birds and the trees, the road and the sky, and a soft bed of daffodils. Then she listened to the sounds and to the beats of the words and phrases, searching for poetic form. But instead of lines of charcoal measured with a ruler, she measured her lines in verse. (33)

This passage—the comparisons to music and the visual arts, the shaping and re-shaping of preliminary "sketches" into the structure of a composition—will resonate with many of today's poets, whether they compose in formal verse or not. The images of Nunhead and the Isle of Wight, however, are specific to Mew's childhood summers, which were spent in the countryside with her brother and sisters.

Charmingly, Pearson intersperses her narrative with references to Mew's own work. Her description of Charlotte (drawn from a surviving photograph) includes the following details:

> Charlotte had the petite figure and heart-shaped face of a fox, which framed large, deep-set eyes as alert as a startled hare's. (13)

It would be hard to read this portrait and *not* recall the lines from Mew's "Farmer's Bride"—

> Shy as a leveret, swift as he,
> Straight and slight as a young larch tree [. . .]
> (ed. Warner, 30-34)

Of course, "The Farmer's Bride"—as Pearson so skillfully proves—is far from the only poem by Charlotte Mew that is worth reading. In the appendix to this volume, Pearson includes two of my personal favorites: "The Changeling" and "Fame," with several others. I hope, as Pearson does, that *Bloomsbury's Late Rose* will inspire modern-day readers to re-visit one of the most exquisite forgotten lesbian poets of the early twentieth century.

Work Cited
Mew, Charlotte. *Collected Poems and Selected Prose.* ed. Val Warner. New York: Routledge, 2003.

Mother-Daughter Banquet: A Memoir
by **Alice Bloch**
Minerva Rising Press, 2019
Paperback, 157 pages, $15.00

Reviewed by Roberta Arnold

In *Mother-Daughter Banquet*, Bloch presents a bird's eye view into the lives of four women who volley the mothering ball back and forth. By way of introduction, Bloch cameos the four in a paragraph for each; the view is in motion, to or from a live performance, with one of the four women in the car with young Alice.

Four overtly different women teach a unique set of skills to their protégée, Alice Bloch. The book is so rich in detail and so well-crafted that it reads more like literary fiction than memoir. In the order of Grandmother, Mother, Stepmother, and Aunt, Bloch delivers these women to us in story form precision.

Beginning near the end of her life, in an assisted-living facility in Florida, Grandma Laura lives with caregivers who guide her through dementia. We then move back in time to Grandma Laura as embellishing raconteur, a larger than life presence whose fun, zany character embodies living life to its fullest by entering center stage, and truth be damned. At Temple Anshe Emeth's annual mother-daughter banquet, dressed as Clarabell the Clown (from the popular *Howdy Doody* show), Grandma Laura engages with an audience of children by squirting them with seltzer water from a shaken bottle. Watching the spectacle from a close distance, so as not to get wet, the child Alice no longer feels the immense sorrow of being motherless. The squeals of enjoyment from the children make Grandma Laura a star, and Alice is suddenly in an enviable position. "We stood by the stage watching Clarabell prance and lunge and take pratfalls. 'That's our Grandmother,' we bragged to the other girls. With Grandma's performance, I felt my status change from that of a pitied orphan to that of a lucky child." (p. 28)

When the subject of Alice's lesbianism comes up with Grandma Laura, the humanity of these female-to-female relationships rises with the times. Bloch writes, "I had always thought Grandma Laura would reject me permanently if she found out I was a lesbian, but when the moment came, her reaction was surprisingly mild. One of her sons, tired of hearing her boast about my brothers and me, told her, 'That wonderful granddaughter of yours is a dyke . . .' I apologized for not having told her sooner, and wrote a long letter of explanation. She called me and said, 'Your letter is so full of love. I keep it on the dining room table, so I can see it all day long.'" (p. 38)

The story of the mother is next. A mother soon to be dying of cancer in the back bedroom. Steeped in traditional Jewish tradition, subscribing to *The Jewish Home Beautiful*, Bloch's mother is remembered through compilation as well as memory. Alice relies on scraps of letters, pictures, stories and an eidetic memory to piece together who her mother was. One day, when Alice faints during her violin lesson—she is not eating during the day at school because she cannot stand the cafeteria food—the mother goes to bat on her behalf. However, the father insists she must eat it anyway. And her mother is overruled.

The Great Depression and Hitler's War, mitigated by the teachings of Jewish Community & Culture, become fodder for rebellion. We see Grandma Laura defying her husband by telling raunchy jokes and laughing, sometimes laughing until it hurts. Alice's mother had enlisted as a WAVE during the war and had sneaked out from her camp at night, much to Alice's delight.

The stepmother, although tightly wound by the expectations of her own mother and the conforming Emily Post lifestyle, does not hide her bold choices: the dark lipsticked cigarette, the liquor, and the chocolate soufflé combine to feed her rebel within, the rebel who prefers the company of women to men. Aunt Ros teaches Alice about adventure, play, and "following the music," whenever time permits—and she does not have to work to put her brother through his education. The life of Aunt Ros stands as an example of life hungrily lived within the restraints of the time. We follow Aunt Ros to her brother's music store in Harlem as she plays the piano in the store with the Jazz greats who come in to enquire about buying a piano, taking off in song, inventing musical riffs between them. Aunt Ros on the piano, in her element.

Through Bloch's essential memory and writing skill, the four lives revivify before our eyes and hum across the pages like song. The unflinching look at all of the lives, including her own, speaks to who we are unadorned in relationship to other women, not solely bound by roles, but enriched by mutual love. Through this cadre of women, Bloch also pays homage to Jewish women who carry forward Jewish culture and mentorship. This is storytelling at its best: heady and emotional territory; a real-life construction of experience moving seamlessly through generations. *The Mother-Daughter Banquet* is as original as it is familiar: a treasury of mother-daughter stories sure to become a lesbian library classic.

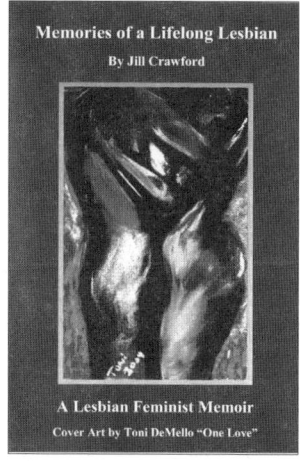

Memories of a Lifelong Lesbian
by **Jill Crawford**
Pink Peony Production, 2019
Paperback, 468 pages, $20

Reviewed by Jean Taylor

Memories of a Lifelong Lesbian is a thoroughly lesbian memoir by an out lesbian, Jill Crawford, about her many lesbian friends and lovers who have given meaning, companionship, and love to her life over the decades.

"It all began with Sister Edmond," Jill writes at the beginning, "my fourth-grade nun. It was 1952 and I was nine years old, living in Chicago . . . I can still see her out in the courtyard, in her robes and habit, running the bases." Sister Edmond was a great role model for a baby dyke. However, Jill and her family, including her younger sister Jackie, soon moved to live not far from her Italian grandparents in the country where her grandfather taught her about farming and carpentry and she worked in the garden with her grandmother. Jill explains her heart was broken and even though "I cried myself to sleep for a month . . . I would just have to see to it myself."

Jill's life over the next several decades—she will turn seventy-six at the end of 2019—is full of diverse experiences. Upon seeing the film *The Children's Hour*, based on Lillian Hellman's play, with her classmates, Jill made an important discovery: "I realised I was not the only Lesbian in the world." After successfully passing her GED exams at the age of eighteen, Jill joined the navy: "Boot camp was an experience I wouldn't wish on anyone." As she had been playing the trumpet since age ten, Jill expected to be able to join the navy band; the sexist regulations wouldn't allow it, although she was allowed to play reveilles in the morning and taps in the evening on her bugle.

Jill went on to study medicine and was assigned to Quonset Point Naval Air Station in Rhode Island, which meant she was able to go to New York on her time off. She frequented coffee houses, "such as the Café Wha, the Café Why Not?, and when we could afford it the Village Gate" where she saw Peter, Paul and Mary perform. Jill's career in medicine was a success and she enjoyed the variety of experiences, including birthing babies and saving lives.

When Jill joined NOW, the National Organisation for Women, and attended a consciousness-raising group in 1973, her approach to life changed completely. Among other things, Jill helped start and worked at a rape crisis hotline in LA and was a member of the Lesbian Task Force 1974 to promote lesbian visibility in NOW. Jill had many jobs over the years, including at an insurance office, at the VA Hospital, and as a realtor: "The main reason I chose to acquire a real estate license in the first place was so that I could be self-employed. I needed a way to make a living while being a Feminist activist. This was my real calling in life . . . What I was really doing was working a full-time job as an activist, and a part-time job to support my activism. There were many Lesbian Feminist Activists who did as I did, in order to promote our cause . . . This was one of the many reasons that the Lesbian was a central force in the Women's Movement."

In her lesbian relationships, Jill excelled, starting in seventh grade at twelve years old with Lynne who "got into bed and started right in kissing me. I never stopped her . . . The practise kissing and our close friendship went on for four years . . . It never evolved into anything more . . . We were learning the art of intimacy."

During her navy training she met Suzie who "puts her arms around me and kisses me. I don't know if it is because I can hardly keep my eyes open, or because it is my first real Lesbian kiss, but I find that I am left speechless. She looks deeply into my tired eyes and says, 'You do know that you are a Lesbian, don't you?' I reply, 'I am now,' and we both laugh." There was Verna "who likes to be called Vern. Of course, she does, she's a real live Lesbian." And Dale who was straight when she met Jill. They go to bed and make love: "We fall asleep wrapped together like braided hair. You can't tell where one body part ends and the other begins. Now, I finally feel like a real Lesbian."

Jill practiced serial monogamy without any painful or disconcerting overlaps, breaking up with one lover, with many grief-stricken months and a year or so in between, before she even considered beginning another relationship; this speaks to her adherence to her personal brand of integrity.

Jill did not always have an easy time of it. She was raped at the age of eighteen and decided not to report it; she was glad for the support of her lesbian friends to get her through. I suspect that it is Jill's sense of humour and the many stories she enjoys telling that make the difference and contribute to her strength.

Of immense importance is the ongoing support of her lesbian community. Jill's fortieth birthday celebration in 1983 included friends from "Sisterhood Bookstore in West LA, Nancy from Page One Books in Pasadena, Carol and Maria from Sojourner

Books in Long Beach and Sandy and I round out that group for Feminist Horizons Gift and Bookstore in West LA."

Finally, at the age of forty-four, Jill met Lynda Taylor at a monthly pot-luck for lesbians aged forty-five and over. Jill had a list of criteria for a potential lover: "I say, 'I can tell you what the first two questions should be.' Lynda says, 'Enlighten us.' I say, 'Number one, are you a Feminist? Number two, are you capable of intimacy?' . . . I make a note to myself, a good sense of humour question #3."

After almost three months of dating, "Lynda invites me to stay the night at her condo . . . I take off my PJs, and we slide into bed. We each think we are the best kissers we've ever known. What a great beginning. It is much easier kissing naked in bed, than it is fully clothed in a car . . . We chat in between orgasms, and then we are off again."

The rest is herstory. With so much in common and very much in love, Jill and Lynda moved to Oregon and started a business, Sisterfields Gourmet and Natural Foods, and a monthly lesbian salon with "great food, good women and interesting entertainment." They also helped start the Women With Wings Feminist Choir and celebrated their fiftieth birthdays in November 1993 with a huge lesbian party. They had a women's library of almost three thousand books, and at Thanksgiving they hosted fifty and up to eighty womyn for a sit-down dinner at home and then the local diner.

In 2008, Lynda was diagnosed with congestive heart failure. They sold the business in 2013 and moved to be nearer to medical facilities and the hospital. Since they legally could, they got married; two years later, in 2016, Lynda passed away. Jill writes, "I didn't think my heart could hurt this much, and still go on beating. Each day when I awake, I am still surprised to be here. I keep thinking there is some magic that will come for me in the night and take me from this agony. I have heard it said that one can die of a broken heart, and I now believe that to be true. I wonder how long this will take."

In the midst of her intense grieving, the election served as a double whammy: "I not only lost Lynda, but I, and the rest of the world, lost our chance to create a better world. Hearing the news that Donald Trump had really won the election was like finding out that there really is a Satan . . . A new catastrophe to deal with."

Before she died, Lynda persuaded Jill to begin writing this memoir. Jill writes, "I am finally beginning to come back to myself in this past year. Writing has been a major factor in my healing." It comes as no surprise that the proceeds from this book go to the June Mazer Lesbian Archives in LA.

Crawford's beloved lesbian community gets the last word: "We need to continue supporting ourselves and our community in whatever ways we are able. This includes volunteerism as well as financial support. Some of us are leaving all or part of our estates to long-time community groups such as The Lesbian Archives, Sinister Wisdom, and the Lesbian Connection. These three groups mentioned have been around from thirty to forty-four years."

This is an honest and revealing lesbian memoir, enhanced by several coloured photos, that needs to be read and savoured as a significant contribution to our Lesbian herstory.

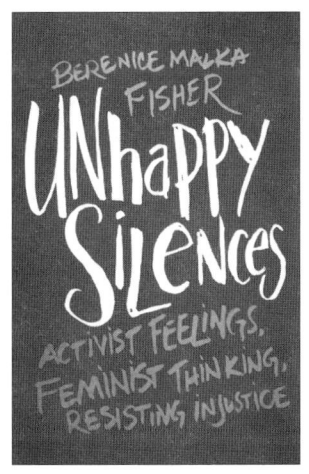

Unhappy Silences: Activist Feelings, Feminist Thinking, Resisting Injustice
by **Berenice Fisher**
Political Animal Press, 2019.
Paperback, 282 pages, $19.50

Review by Carol Anne Douglas

Have you ever kept silent in a political meeting or demonstration when you didn't want to be silent? Of course you have, if you've ever been politically active. As someone who has been silent sometimes to keep from being attacked, especially when I was certain that my point would not carry the day, I was eager to read this book.

Berenice Fisher, professor emerita at New York University, has worked for many years in political groups, including New York City's Women in Black, a mostly Jewish peace group that protests against Israel's treatment of Palestinians, and the lesbian theater ensemble Shock of Grey.

Continuing to feel discomfort about times when she has been silent in political groups, Fisher decided to write about those silences. She aims to help activists learn how to better understand themselves and their groups, and to continue with activism after undergoing challenging experiences. Fisher talked with other activists and studied other activists' writings about times when they have been silent and their analyses of problems in activism. She cites writers like Gloria Anzaldúa, Dorothy Day, Audre Lorde, Martha Nussbaum, and Penny Rosenwasser. At the end of each chapter, Fisher suggests ways we can change unhappy silences into points for discussion.

Although she had long identified with progressive causes, Fisher did not think of herself as a lesbian until she became involved in the second wave of the feminist movement. One of her first political silences occurred when she was in a meeting in which there were a number of out lesbians and one lesbian challenged her to declare her sexual orientation. Still in the throes of considering that, Fisher felt paralyzed. Her inability to respond made her feel inadequate.

But she tried to understand her feelings. If as activists we pathologize negative emotions, our first impulse is to cure or hide them, she says. But negative emotions invite us to raise questions that nest in our unhappy silences, she writes, questions that sometimes merit discussion. The way the woman addressed her was a sign that something was amiss in the group, Fisher says.

Much later, she sometimes felt inadequate during Women in Black's silent protests when observers yelled at the protestors, particularly because the counter-demonstrators often were other Jews who felt that criticizing Israel played into the hands of anti-Semites. Because she realized that some of those who were angry at her had undergone more terrible experiences of anti-Semitism than she had, Fisher never knew whether to try to talk with them or simply listen to them.

Fisher knows from experience that activists can become mired in a sense of demoralization, feeling that they won't be able to change an oppressive situation. Often they escape into depression. If we withdraw from a political group or a meeting, we may feel shame at not being able to handle the situation, Fisher says. She suggests counterbalancing our negative feelings with positive ones, like seeing that even though we were silent, some aspect of the action was successful.

Fisher lived very close to "Ground Zero" at the time of the September 11, 2001 attacks. The toxic air permeated her neighborhood. Fear became more real for her. She attended a peace demonstration in Washington Square a few days after the attack, and felt hopeless and helpless about the nation's militarist response. The feelings of helplessness and isolation are the greatest problems for peace and justice movements, she writes. She tries to confront those feelings as best she can.

Fisher looks at the different possible reactions to terrible events like the 2016 election. She considers "don't mourn, organize" versus "first grieve, then organize." Clearly, she feels more drawn to the latter.

"Terror paralyzes the mind and body," Fisher says, but hope can fill our chest with air and enable our minds to explore.

She also discusses the happiness that we can feel in political activism. We need to understand that the happiness is situational: Circumstances can change. "Our political victories may well include elements of grief," she writes. That does not make them less precious, Fisher says.

Fisher worries that physical frailty as she ages and difficulty with the increasingly electronic media of politics may prevent her from making the kind of political contribution she wants to make, but she was glad that a mostly young group supporting Bernie Sanders's presidential candidacy encouraged her to pass out leaflets. She was pleased to be useful and to have an opportunity to talk to the people who took the leaflets.

This book is wise and profound. I think that anyone who reads it will benefit from it.

My Butch Career: A Memoir
by **Esther Newton**
Duke University Press
November 2018, 288 pages.

Reviewed by Sarah Heying

What's at stake in the academic study of one's self? How to remain fair and honest? How to write of personal matters with the purpose of scholarly contribution in mind? Lesbian feminists have long challenged the limits of what counts as serious scholarship, producing some of the most ground-breaking work in academia and beyond; consider collections like *The Bridge Called My Back* and *Sister Outsider*, which combine poetry, autobiography, philosophy, political theory, and multiple other genres to build fuller, more nuanced pictures of women's lives that are attentive to multiple ways of knowing. Like Audre Lorde, Esther Newton came of age before Stonewall, before the feminist print movement, and before lesbian herstory efforts made glaringly apparent the urgency of archiving the quickly-disappearing stories that have been traditionally barred from our collective annals. Newton published *Mother Camp*, one of the first book-length anthropological studies of gay and trans people in the U.S. (and for a long time, one of the *only* anthropological studies of LGBTQ lives) nearly fifty years ago within an academic field that, as Newton puts it, "is dominated by the romance of the pith helmet." The foundational text inspired the works of Gayle

Rubin, Judith Butler, and numerous other thinkers who found an academic home under the banner of queer studies, yet Newton herself hardly carries the same level of renown as her scholarly progeny. Now, thanks in part to Duke University Press's visionary approach towards scholarship, her work and her name are experiencing a revival of remembrance. Like many queer and lesbian memory-projects, this revival is necessarily part recollection, part invention.

Unlike Lorde, Newton is not a poet but a social scientist by training and a Freudian through therapy. "Half-consciously I associated scholarship with the masculine part of myself that I later called 'the Biographer,' an entity who was nothing but the facts ma'am, with no room for play or creativity." Though she spent nearly a decade abandoning scholarship to mimic the free-association of her literary butch idol, Gertrude Stein, she eventually recognized her talents and predilections lay elsewhere: "Now I have made peace with the Biographer, and she is a butch intellectual who likes to write."

While her ways of remembering reflect some of her fascination with free-association, this memoir is structured in a largely linear, chronological fashion that moves along Freudian stages of psychosexual development. Butch identity for her is "about a gender expression that combines some version of the masculinity that you saw around you as a child with same-sex desire." She insists that she inherited her butchiness from her charismatic yet ethically dubious adoptive father and overbearing mother as much as she did from New York's bar dyke scene. "Well, we invent ourselves," she writes, "but just not as we please." This memoir may not sit well with anyone skeptical of origin stories or broad-strokes psychological claims, but what's clear is that Newton's survival depended on them. From her parents, she counts among her inheritances a string of complexes, but also a rebellious streak, a "strong constitution," and a "native intelligence." From her lovers, she inherits the power of self-creation, as with

Betty Silver, who appeared as if "she were acting in a lesbian movie that didn't exist yet."

The Butch Biographer can sound a bit crotchety at times, especially in her frequent references to "today young queers" (with "queer" often appearing in quotes), her disdain for graffiti, and an understanding of trans identities that is fairly lacking in nuance. She also breeds show dogs and can be caught making comparisons between women and her four-legged projects: "The beauty of certain purebred dogs floors me. I am devastated, thrilled, as before the shape and movements of certain feminine women." Newton doesn't strike me as someone people might describe as humble, especially with the admission that she has often "wondered about people who seem defeated by circumstances less daunting" than hers. The perception that her experiences of victimization are extraordinary seems warranted given the extreme misogyny and homophobia she faced in a fiercely male-dominated field, but also quite exasperating when coupled with her slips into elitism and bravado.

Case in point: in discussing feminism with a friend and colleague of her French lover (a lover Newton describes earlier as speaking in "excellent but accented British English"), she recalls that the friend explained "what I already knew: that according to Freud, women could never be liberated, because we would always be blocked by envy." She describes the six-year relationship with this Frenchwoman as a primarily political project (I'm reminded of the project of training show dogs), and she offers up fairly flippant interpretations of the politics of Jill Johnston, Monique Wittig, and her other radical pals. She's a boastful butch, but at the end of the day I'd rather hear more women bragging about themselves than not.

For all Freud's faults, he gives Newton a language for accepting her faults and mistakes and moving forward with a clearer purpose of who she wants to be. When reflecting on the problematic threads of her masculinity, she returns to her origin story, to a fight between her mother and father: "I didn't want to be like her, standing in the corner, screaming. I wanted to be like him, dominant and scary." Dealing with her own misogyny becomes an imperative part of her journey towards self-acceptance, just as it is for most women and lesbians, both butch and otherwise. The truth of the matter is that it is still difficult for a visibly butch woman to have a stable professional life, and that was even more so the case fifty years ago. Between Freud and the bar dykes, Newton learned how to articulate herself into a life worth living. Call it pompous, call it brave.

So what's at stake for Newton and her story? One of the most prestigious university presses in the country published a memoir by a self-named butch lesbian and listed it in their anthropology section. Not bad for an anthropologist whom Margaret Mead once told would never be a "real anthropologist" until she studied foreigners. Newton once again breaks ground in her field and beyond by suggesting that anthropological methods might be better directed towards the self. For an artsy, intellectual butch like me, her memoir lives inside me just as Gertrude Stein and the "warm hands, light-blue eyes, musical French voice" of her lover all live together in her "brain and blood." She's a bit boastful, and she's also my fearless butch auntie.

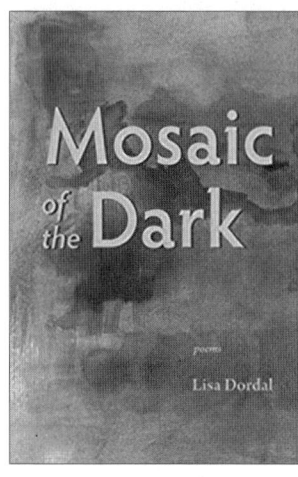

Mosaic of the Dark
By **Lisa Dordal**
Black Lawrence Press, 2017
74 pages, paperback, $15.95

Reviewed by Sara Gregory

Lisa Dordal's first full-length poetry collection, *Mosaic of the Dark*, transforms the tenants of a male-centric faith into an authentic portrait of a young lesbian woman as she navigates not only a coming out, but also a coming into herself. With each chapter—Commemoration, Holy Week, Matrimonies, Survival, Testament, This Is Praying, Mosaic of the Dark—Dordal leans into the pillars of her relationship with God as imbricated with family, sexuality, and gender presentation. Striking are the ways by which Dordal traces the origins of her own closeted mother's ideologies on sexuality and marriage, peeling back the layers of her tense family life to reveal repressed desires and a culture of silence. Recalling her own childhood playing Mary at a Christmas pageant, Dordal's first poem establishes the collection's resistance to the patriarchal aspects of her faith, while simultaneously revealing the inseparability of her identity from her relationship to God:

> Everyone said I made a great Mary.
> That I did a great job being
> the one God descended upon. No,
> not descended upon. Entered.
> That I did a great job being the one

God entered. And who
afterward called it holy (3).

Childhood, maturity, and identity are frequently woven together as Dordal parallels her deviation from the traditional and the heterosexual with early attempts to mimic just exactly that via schoolyard games and uncomfortable dates. In "Sixth Grade" Dordal describes being married off to a classmate during recess. The officiator, a classmate named Peter, told her: "there were two types / of women: / that I was the kind men married / not the kind men used for practicing" (21). The irony that Dordal and her classmates *were* practicing is not lost on readers, even as Dordal delves deeper into the external pressures placed on lesbian women and questioning children to conform and conceal. What's so interesting here is Dordal's willingness to expose the early replication and mimicry of the wider society of adults, especially as tied to God and meaningful, heterosexual unions. "Wedding" draws from such memories as every preparation of the past seeks to constrain Dordal's desires and future:

Grandmother, mother,
daughter—there in that moment of keeping

and quiet, quiet breaking. And the Gospel—
slinked in by the preacher—an appeal
to the rightness of the past, as I said "I do"

with almost every cell and, in the process,
began the long and tight-lipped death
of my mother, who taught me how (25).

Again, the psychic and generational sacrifice of conformity are revealed through the tight-lipped deaths and quiet breakings of Dordal's mother and grandmother. Throughout the collection, it is often Dordal's own complicated relationship with her mother that truly drives the recasting of the God. The dramatic center of *Mosaic of the Dark* rests within Dordal's romantic and sexual desire other women, but also in her desire to understand the silences of her mother, the divinity of that deemed insignificant in scripture. Writing, "I know what it's like not to be seen; what it's like to be smoothed over by discourse . . . a dark, holy heaviness lost: /the year I taught New Testament . . . and everyone thought I was straight," it is apparent that Dordal actively engages with aspects of her faith as the perilous, beautiful, inescapable parts of a greater whole (41). Yet despite her struggles, Dordal finds ways to rearticulate her spirituality, embracing her religion and God while still resisting those aspects which would deny her value or existence, or that of her mother and family's. She celebrates the divinity of houseflies, transforms what it means to pray, finds compassion from an openly gay priest, and uses "kissing energy" to safely travel the deep south with her lover.

Mosaic of the Dark invites readers to begin their own deep reckonings with figures that sometimes wear the same face: God and mother, family and oppressor, games and conformity. Dordal delivers a meditative, convincing collection that creatives a whole of moments both dark and light.

JANICE GOULD — A REMEMBRANCE

My friend Janice Gould is gone, yet her presence haunts my heart and mind. As I sit at my desk, surrounded by her books, by photographs I've made of her over the years, by the grateful memory of our recent goodbye, I hear her voice straining against the spurts of pain, feel the ebbing life beneath my hand on her skin.

Margaret Randall and Janice Gould in 2010

*

Janice Gould (1949-2019) was a poet's poet, that is, a poet who was meticulous in her craft yet continued searching for that place where authenticity takes up residence in the poem. Her solutions came to her, "chose her," as she often said. They bore the marks of her Indian and lesbian identities and her delight with the smallest images and acts. In her best poems she spoke in a uniquely personal yet socially aware voice.

Janice was also many other things: a perceptive and profoundly moving essayist; a professor of women's and ethnic studies[1] who never stopped learning herself and so constantly offered her students new ideas and challenged them to push those ideas further; a person of Koyangk'auwi (Koncow) Maidu and European descent whose childhood was rife with racism and who ultimately explored her mixed blood heritage in both poetry and prose; a working-class woman who wrote convincingly about laboring in canneries before finding her never entirely comfortable niche in academia; a lesbian who struggled with familial preconceptions and prejudices growing up and then was called upon much later in life to understand and accept her trans father coming out as Cynthia in his seventies; a talented musician and skilled martial artist; an excellent photographer and good friend. She made a longtime life with soulmate and librarian Mimi Wheatwind whom, although they married when it was legal to do so, she always referred to lovingly as "my best friend." Together they reveled in family, gardens, poetry, and handmade books.

Janice's five major poetry collections—*Beneath My Heart*, *Earthquake Weather*, *Doubters and Dreamers*, *The Force of Gratitude*, and *Seed*—have endeared her to readers, and I believe that as a body of work they will be studied far into the future as evidence of an exceptional history and sensibility among the explosion of dynamic women's voices in the last half of the twentieth century and first decades of the twenty-first. Her brilliant essays often add context to her poems, and also reach out to embrace and promote the work of other writers.[2]

---

1 Janice stopped working as she became too ill to teach and left the University of Colorado at Colorado Springs as an Associate Professor Emerita.

2 Among Janice's many insightful essays are "Poems as Maps in American Indian Women's Writing" in *Speak to Me Words: Essays on Contemporary American Indian Poetry*, edited by Dean Rader and Janice Gould, University of Arizona Press, Tucson, 2003; and "My Father, Cynthia Conway" in *A Journal of Lesbian and Gay Studies*, Vol. 16, Num 1-2, Duke University Press, Durham, North Carolina, 2010.

Beneath My Heart was Janice's breakthrough collection.[3] It has also somehow disappeared from my library, something I noticed as I was writing this piece. I have all her other books. After repeatedly returning to bookshelves and looking behind books without luck, I had to recur to our university library. It is with a copy from its holdings that I am able to reread this strong first book.

Beneath My Heart is essentially about family, biological and chosen, but hardly conventional in tone or content. The opening poem, "Coyotismo," begins with the lines: "My mother lay on her side to birth me. / This was millennia ago / when the earth was still fresh / with the energy of being" (11). But this image of warm fecundity immediately becomes a litany of angry pronouncements, powerful in their unrelenting rage:

> I was here first.
> If any came before me
> they were lies and unwanted [. . .]
>
> We were poor. I was cold.
> Mama made me a coat but no trousers.
> People laughed at me [. . .]
>
> They joked about my sex,
> said nasty things about my genitalia.
> I became vengeful.
>
> Once I heard the moon whisper behind my back.
> I scooped hot coals
> and threw them in her fat face.
> Sure, it burned my hands—
> but she is marked with permanent surprise.

---

3   *Beneath My Heart*, Firebrand Books, Ithaca, New York, 1990.

This powerful first poem is followed by others. "Autobiography" begins: "I was born of a half-breed mother / and a transvestite father / on all Fools' Day / in the year of forty-nine" (19). The extraordinary "History Lesson" traces her tribal history from 1832 to 1984, extrapolating from the collective degradation of colonialism to how that degradation plays itself out in the life of a single child (28–32). And this rage continues throughout the collection. Even in later poems, such as "The Woman I Love Most" (46) and "I Am Loved for My Beauty" (56), there is more indignation than other emotions. And then, slowly, the mood changes to a hard-won hope. In "Looking for Chamita" Janice evokes Ansel Adams's famous photograph "Moon Over Hernandez" (62). The poem ends with the lines: "Our dream history has become possible / in this least of all possible worlds."

Six years would pass before Janice's next book, *Earthquake Weather*.[4] It opens with a preface in the form of an essay by the poet about her origins and early life. It is unusual for a book of poems to begin with such explanation and does not seem like something Janice would have thought of inserting. Perhaps it was suggested by the publisher. The University of Arizona Press was developing Sun Tracks, an American Indian Literary Series devoted to Native authors, and may have believed those autobiographical lines would help provide an underpinning for what followed.[5]

---

[4] *Earthquake Weather*, University of Arizona Press, Tucson, 1996.

[5] At a time when certain categories of women writers were ignored by mainstream publishing, specialized presses brought out the work of Native American, African-American, Hispanx, and lesbian authors, among others. The intention and results have been double-edged in my opinion. On the one hand, we have books by many extraordinary writers who might otherwise not have been published. On the other, the effort encapsulated many of these writers, much as the term "women writers" did in previous generations. Janice Gould was a remarkable poet who explored all sorts of themes in her work, not simply a remarkable woman poet or lesbian poet or Indian poet. I am grateful to some of the vibrant lesbian publishers, such as Firebrand, that brought out Janice's first major collection, *Beneath My Heart*. It published one of my books as well. I would also like to see a general interest house reedit and really market all of Janice's work.

In this book the poet has distilled her experience, using it with more nuance, yet just as powerfully. Although the poems in this volume certainly stand alone, the preface is also rich and rewarding: we learn of a particular landscape and the family members who inhabit it. Following many evocative memories, Janice writes: "The displacement and dissolution of my Indian family represents one aspect of the colonization that took place in northern California" (xi). She expands that statement in observations of the everyday.

Janice never got bogged down in clichéd political rhetoric. She rendered the political as something the reader could touch and feel. Many of her poems take memory and thread it through the needle's eye of one Indian lesbian woman poet's sensibility, making it as intimate as it is socially conscious and universal. For example, "What Happened to My Anger"[6] is among the many powerful poems in *Earthquake Weather*. Here it is:

> What happened to my anger?
> It was rounded up
> and removed to a camp.
> Or went into self-exile.
> Or perhaps it painted itself white.
> Now it goes into the world
> with a happy face.
>
> What happened to my anger?
> It turned into a worm
> coiled in my belly.
> It formed into a mass of cold cells
> attached to my spleen.
> It became the wound in my hand.

---

6 Op cit., 8.

What happened to my anger?
It became a eunuch
and laid itself down on the divan
before the flickering TV,
drowning its sorrow

in vacuity.
It went to the kitchen in search of food,
prepared many meals.
It cleaned the toilet,
the catbox,
the carpet.

My anger has not worn itself out.
It has not become obedient,
but dumb.

Janice Gould and Mimi Wheatwind, her spouse and best friend

In contrast with the anger poetry in *Beneath My Heart*, in this poem the anger is still there, explicit and brutal, but a slight softening seems to have taken place.

Earthquake Weather also includes a poem about Janice's father who became a trans woman late in life. In "My Father" (43–44) she repeatedly asks: "As a woman, is my father beautiful?," positing the question as a leitmotif introducing stanzas in which she evokes her fear of his unpredictability, her lifelong confusion at his attitudes of disregard for her own personhood, and his demand that she keep the secrets that mattered to him. This poem, referencing a subject Janice returns to often over the years, retains a central place in Janice's work.

Also published in the Sun Tracks series is Janice's third full-length collection *Doubters and Dreamers* in 2011.[7] In this volume Janice continues exploring the landscape and context of her past. The first poem, "Indian Mascot" (1–2), opens with the lines:

> Now begins the festival and rivalry of late fall,
> the weird debauch and daring debacle
>
> of frat-boy parties as students parade foggy streets in mock
> processions, bearing on shoulders scrawny effigies of dead,
> defeated Indians cut from trees, where,
> in the twilight, they had earlier been hung.
>
> "Just dummies," laughs our dad, "Red Indians hung
> or burned—it's only in jest." [. . .]

In "Renegade" (3–4) the poet declares: "Mama was no reservation squaw. Abandoned / but not disowned, she married white and went back home / only when the tank was full, smoking

---

7 *Doubters and Dreamers*, University of Arizona Press, Tucson, 2011.

at a steady fifty / up the river road, taking each snake-eye turn in stride." Other poems in this collection continue to delve into a past in which Indian identity and white assimilation trouble one another. It is in this book, too, that Janice begins to intersperse her poetry with prose texts, a practice that continues in her next collections.

In *The Force of Gratitude*[8] the doubters and dreamers are no longer separate beings but are acknowledged within the same body, often that of the poet herself. Here is a poem called "The Girl I Used to Be" (3). Like other texts in this book, prose pieces as well as poems, it links childhood memories with a difficult adult acceptance of self. The first half of the first stanza and entire last stanza of this poem are especially moving to me:

> I was the girl who backed into life,
> got lost, then disappeared again
> under tables and in drawers,
> between unused tools hung
> on dusty pegs, among red lines
> etched on imaginary maps. [. . .]
>
> [. . .] I was the girl who seldom spoke,
> who slept alone fully clothed, ready to bolt
> into the startled dawn. Then one day
> enticed by stones, this girl plunged into
> a clear Sierra stream and rose, gasping
> from that brutal creek, terrified,
> but absolutely clean.

I could reproduce dozens of Janice's poems and still fail to give a sense of the fullness of her voice. But I will offer one more,

---

8 *The Force of Gratitude*, Headmistress Press, Sequim, Washington, 2017.

the first in her final collection, *Seed*,[9] completed just before, but published after, her tragic cancer diagnosis.[10] Several poems in this book seem to me to hold an awareness of what she would soon be called upon to endure. This is simply titled "A Poem" (1–2), and I transcribe it in full:

A Poem

is about to flower
full force from my abdomen,
my spleen, my wrists,
my ankles. I could feel
the pip of it in last night's dream
that kept threading its way
back to sacred land, where

I found myself in my twenties,
and where, later, you and I
were dream-happy. Our house,
the one that appears in all
the strange locals you and I
dream-inhabit, could be seen
dimly through the pines
on a dry hillside. Our landlady
was there, stooping over her garden.
We are always moving in

---

9   *Seed*, Headmistress Press, Sequim, Washington, 2019.

10 In an interview for SAIL, Studies in American Indian Literatures, completed just before Janice's death, she told professor and friend Ruth Salvaggio: "I didn't know, when I started *Seed*, that I would be faced with a terminal illness as fall changed to winter last year [. . .] Maybe psychically I 'knew' something was manifesting inside me when I wrote [the book], but I was still feeling physically healthy. I did know, however, that I needed a few days by myself [. . .]. As I read back through Seed, I see that some of the poems are concerned with death."

or moving away from that
falling-down place made of stone,
or weathered wood, or adobe.
But just passing by our old home
as I did in last night's dream
made me feel excited—yes,
there it is!—and serene,
like seeing an old friend.
And when I woke, I longed
for that familiar dreamscape,
as if it is a real land, as if
that dark earth the landlady turns
with her trowel is scented
with loam, is mapped with leaves
and small roots, as if the wind
blowing dust down the mountain road
is an actual wind, as if a poem
could emerge from a seed.

Reading this poem, I felt that writing it Janice, perhaps more intuitively than explicitly, saw herself as a seed: born, dying and re-emerging upon the landscape she explored with such intimate precision.

Janice herself has said that "The poems that feel most real to me are the ones where the words feel like they've chosen me. The 'choosing' I do is intuitive; it isn't simply an intellectual process. Clearly the poem will have a final line, just as it will have a title and a first line—and content. Learning where and what those things are has to do with learning and practicing the craft. I think it's mysterious, that 'choosing.'"[11]

---

[11] Taken from a pre-publication version of the interview with Ruth Salvaggio.

Janice Gould and Mimi Wheatwind in 1990

*

The foregoing biographic, bibliographic, and professional information falls short of portraying Janice as she was—to students, colleagues, and friends. Her insatiable curiosity about language enabled her to learn songs in several, accompanying herself on guitar or accordion as she sang with perfect accent. Her intellectual courage was legion. Her warm humor and genuine interest in others created room for exchanges that made all those she touched richer. We belonged to a group of women writers that met for more than five years in the 1980s and '90s.[12] Her thoughtful comments about my work always helped me to make it better. When I taught at Trinity College in Hartford, Connecticut,

---

12 We met monthly at the home of one of the participants. The host provided a main dish and others brought salad, drinks, bread, dessert. We always marveled that, without prior arrangement, we never ended up with four loaves of bread or other such duplications. Janice is not the first member of that beautiful collective to have left us; Paula Gunn Allen and Patricia Clark Smith are also no longer here in body.

I invited Janice to perform in a reading series I called "Rainbow Sound." Local poets from several ethnic communities opened for important female poets of color who came from across the country. The well-known poet often read at an area school or appeared in a Trinity classroom. I still remember the impact of Janice's formal reading. The audience at Trinity was not accustomed to hearing poetry that made the American Indian experience so explicit, so present. I also remember Janice's generosity with my students as she shared intimate pieces of her life.

When Janice and Mimi left Albuquerque to take jobs—first in Portland, Oregon and then in Colorado Springs—it was a great loss to our community. But Janice had a sister, Lindsay, living in northern New Mexico and they returned to visit every now and then. I never felt they were far away. I included poems by Janice in an anthology of twelve US American poets published in Mexico and received messages of appreciation from many Mexican readers.[13] And I would often find a "poem of the day" or "poem of the week" in my email inbox, sent by Mimi.

When, in November of 2018, Janice wrote to say she had been diagnosed with pancreatic cancer, it was a shock. As is too often the case with this form of the illness, by the time it was named it was implacably advanced. Most tribute pieces shy away from dwelling on the subject's final illness, but I feel that the way Janice dealt with hers was so much a part of who she was that I must speak of it, if only briefly. She and Mimi shared the terrible news, then periodically updated the medical prognosis as well as news of Janice's ever more limited radius of activity. She herself was also practical, mentioning meeting with Human Services on her campus in order to establish the benefits Mimi would need when she was gone.

---

13 *12 poetas: antología de nuevos poetas estadounidenses*, La Herata Feliz, MarEs DeCierto Ediciones, and Mexico's Secretaría de Cultura, Mexico City, 2017.

Janice seemed optimistic until that was no longer possible: observant of the beauty of a particular bird's song in her yard or the beginnings of the Colorado spring. Her messages were filled with hope, but they were also realistic. Shortly before she died, she sent me three new poems in which she spoke of the ravages the disease was making on her body; the language of those poems was brutal, poignant. One line in particular, in which she speaks of "tumor fevers," has haunted me. Her strong belief that she would be going to meet ancestors who were waiting to embrace her offered a confidence and grace.

Janice Gould

Janice's spirit remained strong and luminous to the end. A fierce will to live was tempered by her acceptance of the inevitable. On June 23, driving down from Boulder where I had been teaching at Naropa University's Summer Writing Program, my wife Barbara and I stopped in Colorado Springs to say goodbye. Janice was already quite weak, but Mimi had assured us she wanted to see us. Our visit only lasted a few minutes. We knew it would be our last. Our conversation was sparse but our feelings intense. It was a privilege to be able to kiss our friend and tell her that we loved her. And a privilege of equal weight to be able to embrace Mimi.

Janice died five days later.

We remember her as a fierce and gentle warrior, a woman of great talent and conviction, a spirit gone much too soon. Her work is her legacy.

Margaret Randall
Albuquerque, July 2019

Family and friends of Janice Gould have established a memorial scholarship in her name at the University of Colorado Colorado Springs. This fund will support UCCS undergraduate student work centered on a Native and/or Indigenous worldview that embraces a way of consciousness that emphasizes the dignity of all living things, respect, humility, gratitude, and the interconnections of all life. People interested in making a contribution to the Janice M. Gould Memorial Scholarship Fund may do so online at https://giving.cu.edu/fund/janice-m-gould-memorial-scholarship-fund.

JANICE GOULD BIBLIOGRAPHY

Books
Seed. Sequim, WA: Headmistress Press, 2019.

The Force of Gratitude. Sequim, WA: Headmistress Press, 2017.

Doubters and Dreamers. Tucson: University of Arizona Press, 2011.

Earthquake Weather: Poems. Tucson: University of Arizona Press, 1996.

Alphabet. Vashon Island, WA: May Day Press, 1996.

Beneath My Heart: Poetry. Ithaca, NY: Firebrand Books, 1990.

Edited Collections
A Generous Spirit: Selected Work by Beth Brant. Dover, FL: Sinister Wisdom; Toronto, Canada: Inanna Publications, 2019.

Essays on Contemporary Indigenous Poetry. Edited with Dean Rader. Tucson: The University of Arizona Press, 2003.

Essays
"Lesbian landscape." *Journal of Lesbian Studies* 20, no. 3–4 (2016). 342–351. https://doi.org/10.1080/10894160.2016.1145486

"Singing, Speaking, and Seeing a World." In *Placing the Academy: Essays on Landscape, Work, and Identity*, edited by Sinor Jennifer and Kaufman Rona, 254–68. University Press of Colorado, 2007. doi:10.2307/j.ctt4cgq72.20.

"Telling Stories to the Seventh Generation: Resisting the Assimilationist Narrative of *Stiya*." In *Reading Native American Women: Critical/Creative Representations*, edited by Inés Hernández-Avila, 9–20. Lanham, MD: Altamira Press, 2005.

"American Indian Women's Poetry: Strategies of Rage and Hope" in *Signs: Journal of Women in Culture and Society*. Vol. 20, No. 4 (Summer, 1995): 797–817. https://doi.org/10.1086/495022

"Postcolonial, Emergent, and Indigent Feminism." *Signs* 20, no. 4 (1995).

"Disobedience (in language) in texts by lesbian Native Americans." In *Ariel* 25, no. 1 (1994): 32–44.

"A Maidu in the City of Gold: Some Thoughts on Censorship and American Indian Poetry." In *The Colour of Resistance: A Contemporary Collection of Writing by Aboriginal Women*, edited by Connie Fife. Toronto: Sister Vision, 1993.

"The Problem of Being 'Indian': One Mixed-Blood's Dilemma." In *De/Colonizing the Subject: The Politics of Gender in Women's Autobiography*, edited by Sidonie Smith and Julia Watson. Minneapolis: University of Minnesota Press, 1992.

"Speaking a World into Existence." *The Women's Review of Books* 9, no. 10/11 (1992): 12. doi:10.2307/4021318.

Numerous anthologies include Gould's poetry such as *The Aunt Lute Anthology of U.S. Women Writers* (edited by Lisa Maria Hogeland and Mary Klages. San Francisco: Aunt Lute Books, 2004); *A Gathering of Spirit: A Collection by North American Indian Women* (edited by Beth Brant. Ithaca: Firebrand Books, 1988); *An Intimate Wilderness: Lesbian Writers on Sexuality* (edited by Judith Barrington. Portland: Eighth Mountain Press, 1991); *Living the Spirit: A Gay American Indian Anthology* (edited by Will Roscoe and Gay American Indians. New York: St. Martin's Press, 1988); *Making Face, Making Soul = Haciendo Caras: Creative and Critical Perspectives by Feminists of Color* (edited by Gloria Anzaldúa. San Francisco: Aunt Lute Foundation Books, 1990); *Native Voices: Indigenous American Poetry, Craft, and Conversations* (edited by CMarie Fuhrman and Dean Rader. North Adams: Tupelo Press,

2019); *Reinventing the Enemy's Language: Contemporary Native Women's Writing of North America* (edited by Joy Harjo and Gloria Bird. New York: W. W. Norton & Co., 1998); *Sovereign Erotics: A Collection of Two-Spirit Literature* (edited by Qwo-Li Driskill, Daniel Health Justice, Deborah A. Miranda, and Lisa Tatonetti. Tucson: University of Arizona Press, 2011); and *Unsettling America: An Anthology of Contemporary Multicultural Poetry* (edited by Maria M. Gillan and Jennifer Gillan. New York: Penguin Books, 1994).

Compiled by Amy Hong.

SNAPSHOT LESBIAN LOVE CELEBRATION

This segment celebrates the love of Joan Nestle & Di Otto: a partnership song sure to reverberate in your bones. Like whorls of upturned sand catching the light and glistening beneath deep waters, this homage of love is another stunning array of brilliant links in the treasures of Sisterhood. (Roberta Arnold)

For Di Otto.

Ten years have passed since I crossed the seas. Ten years of work and play and then so much loss. Now I hold the renewed passport in my hand. All because of you, because you insist on hope, a hope that sings in your upturned phrases, that sits perched on your backpack sharing its bumpy ride down the streets of Havana, London, Melbourne, New York, Beijing, Mumbai. You make a home in whatever city your work takes you to, your true home being the ideas that shape your vision of a world more equitable in its securities while still thriving with difference. Wherever there is a desk, you live. I have watched you work, my black slippery coat with its gold dragon draped around your shoulders, books and papers piled around you as, hour after hour, you read through texts, always looking for insights that will move your work along. The huge shadows of your antagonists hover over you, the governments and the banks, the soldiers and the courts all pitted against the fall of your hennaed hair, the squareness of your words. I turn to look again as I go back into my room to put my own words on paper, and see the frail strength of the future, your comrades, like yourself, chipping away at the stolid face of unquestioned, unquestioning, power. I am afraid to leave what I know, to leave my home. I am afraid to take my body with all its fumbles and mysteries into countries where I have never lived. And then you lay me down and laugh gently in my ear. "You funny old thing," you say and carry me away across the seas into new histories.

Joan Nestle, 1998.

For Joan Nestle.

Twenty-one years later you have used that passport many times, your body criss-crossing continents and hemispheres with its wonders as well as its fumbles. We have made our home together here in Melbourne Australia since 2002, after providing immigration officials with so much archival evidence of our desire for each other that they awarded you permanent residency (as my partner) without interrogating us face-to-face, as is the usual practise. While we are grateful for this recognition of our relationship, we are also keenly aware that we have been granted a privilege that is denied to so many people, particularly people of colour, in far more desperate situations than our own. The coming together of our different sexual histories—you the "'50s fem" and me a product of '70s sexual liberation/lesbian feminism—has taught me that sexualities are indeed historically located and produced, that desire has so many forms and manifestations, and there is so much yet to explore and discover. You astound me with your readings of the world, of politics and of power, from the starting point of the body—and teach me to think about my human rights advocacy even more critically by grounding it in bodies, and in the material histories and archives of the everyday. The "funny old thing" of our pillow talk has more courage and strength than you realise. You carry us both along with your refusal of domesticity and distrust of power, as well as your determination to give almost anything "a go," including loving me.

Di Otto, July 2019

Joan Nestle (left) and Di Otto, 2018, Anglesea

CONTRIBUTORS

Jennifer Abod is a filmmaker, former radio news and feature producer, talk show host, and second-wave lesbian feminist activist, singer, and songwriter. Jennifer began writing poems in grade school and picked it up again when she first fell in love with a woman in her twenties, and again in 2010 when her long-time partner and wife, Dr. Angela Bowen (1936–2018), was diagnosed with Alzheimer's. With a PhD in Intercultural Media Education and Women's Studies, she taught at U Mass Boston, Worcester State, and Hofstra Universities in departments of Communication and Women's Studies. She is a former UCLA Women's Research Scholar. Her award-winning films include: *The Edge of Each Other's Battles: The Vision of Audre Lorde*, *The Passionate Pursuits of Angela Bowen*, *Look Us in the Eye: The Old Women's Project*, and *Nice Chinese Girls Don't: a poetry memoir with Kitty Tsui*. www.jenniferabod.com

Roberta Arnold is a child of the second wave, now a newly-defined crone in the tribe of radical lesbian feminists who embrace LGBTQQIAAP community with the tidal pull. She embraces *Sinister Wisdom* in much the same way: as a well-tended canoe steering us through the years row by row, knowing we are the oars.

Kristy Lin Billuni is a writer of sexy, triumphant stories and teacher of bold, free, turned-on writers. She has aroused thousands of writers in her day job as The Sexy Grammarian and has roots in the sex industry and queer political activism. Her fiction appears in several anthologies and journals, and a handful of theaters, community spaces, and cabaret stages have produced her short plays. She lives with her wife in San Francisco, where she haunts cafes, chases pigeons, and prefers to take the bus.

Wendy Judith Cutler is a radical teacher, writer, and Jewish lesbian feminist and queer activist. She was born in Los Angeles and politicized in the Bay Area, and taught writing and women's studies in Oregon before immigrating to Canada. She resides on Salt Spring Island, BC (the unsurrendered territory of the Coast Salish) with her lovergirl of thirty-three years, Corrie, and their constellation of intimates. She co-authored *Writing Alone Together: Journalling in a Circle of Women for Creativity, Compassion and Connection* (2014) and edited *Finding Home: Collected Stories from Salt Spring Island Circles of Women* (2018). Her play *An Interrogation Story in One-Act* was recently performed and is part of her memoir *An Undutiful Daughter*. She creates sacred circles of women (and queers) writing together. womenwritingwjc.wordpress.com

Shivani Davé is a queer femme educator, artist, and lover of plants, food, magic, and rituals of healing. Her art seeks to queer what appears to be the mundane, routine, day-to day and build connection through that exposure. She is based in NYC where she teaches full-time and writes, collages, utilizes Instagram (@getyouashiv) as a platform for self-publishing, trains in Muay Thai, and gardens part-time. She earned her BA in biochemistry from Vassar College and her MA in teaching from Relay Graduate School of Education. She hopes to continue to work at the intersection of queerness, education, art, and biochemistry.

Carol Anne Douglas worked on the staff of the feminist news journal off our backs from 1973 to 2008, when it ceased publication. She also has taught Feminist Theory at George Washington University. She has written a book on feminist theory, *Love and Politics: Radical Feminist and Lesbian Theories*, and novels in which Lancelot is a woman in disguise and a lesbian (*Lancelot: Her Story* and *Lancelot and Guinevere*).

Jillian Rochelle Etheridge is a teacher from Mississippi. She earned her MA in creative writing and her BFA in theatre from the University of Southern Mississippi. Her work can be found in publications such as *Mississippi's Best Emerging Poets*, *Product Magazine*, and *Apocrypha and Abstractions*. Her short story "Miranda" made *Glimmer Train*'s Sept/Oct 2016 Honorable Mentions list.

Suzanne Feldman received a master's in creative writing from Johns Hopkins University. Her novel *Absalom's Daughters* (Holt, 2016) received a starred review in *Kirkus*. Her short story "The Witch Bottle" was nominated for a Pushcart Prize. She received a Nebula Award and the Editors' Prize for Fiction at *The Missouri Review*. She was a finalist for the Bakeless Prize and was recently accepted as a Dakin Fellow to the Sewanee Writers Conference.

Mo Fowler is a professional gardener and antiques dealer in Chicago, IL where she practices her parallel parking and eavesdrops from her first-floor apartment onto the street below. Her writing can be found in *Not Very Quiet*, *Motley Mag*, *Zone 3 Magazine*, and *Words Dance*. Find her at maureenclaudette.com & follow along @original_mo_fo.

Elizabeth Galoozis is a poet and librarian living in Los Angeles. Her poetry has been published in *Faultline* and *Not Very Quiet*. Her scholarly and critical work have been published in *The Library Quarterly*, *In the Library with the Lead Pipe*, *Amherst Magazine*, *Library Juice Press*, and *ACRL Press*.

Marilyn Hacker is the author of fourteen books of poems, most recently *Blazons* (Carcanet Press, UK, 2019), and including *A Stranger's Mirror* (Norton, 2015) and *Names* (Norton, 2010), the essay collection *Unauthorized Voices* (Michigan, 2010), and sixteen collections of translations of French and francophone poets including Emmanuel Moses, Marie Étienne, Vénus Khoury-Ghata, and Habib Tengour. *DiaspoRenga,* a collaborative book written with the Palestinian-American poet Deema Shehabi, was published by Holland Park Press in 2014. She received the 2009 PEN Award for Poetry in Translation and the International Argana Prize for Poetry from the Beit as-Sh'ir/House of Poetry in Morocco in 2011. She lives in Paris.

Sarah Heying is a PhD Student in English at the University of Mississippi researching the aesthetics of lesbian literature, and especially southern lesbian literature. Her writing has appeared in *Bitch*, *Lambda Book Review*, *The Greensboro Review*, *Ellipsis*, *Broken Pencil*, and elsewhere. She and her partner, Nora Augustine, have a premonition that they'll land teaching jobs at a small liberal arts college in Texas after they finish their PhDs.

Gloria Keeley is a graduate of San Francisco State University with a BA and MA in creative writing. In the 1970s, she was editor and founder of *WOMEN*, a literary journal that was sponsored by the Women's Center, San Francisco State University. Thanks to one of her teachers, Sally Gearhart, many women writers visited the campus. The visitor Keeley remembers the most was Rita Mae Brown. Gloria had just finished reading "Rubyfruit Jungle" and was inspired to hear her talk so articulately and humorously. Keeley's work has appeared in *Spoon River Poetry Review*, *Slipstream*, *The Emerson Review*, and other journals.

Fallen Kittie is an Afro-L'nu queer scholar who studies existentialism and supernatural folklore. She holds degrees in sociology and gender studies and hopes to promptly finish her interdisciplinary doctorate further down the line—in between movie marathons and indie reviews on her website. Although she's always liked to write, she only thought to pursue publication during her undergrad after one of her professors inspired her to critically consider the realms of cinema and the senses.

Claudia Lars (1899–1974), literary pseudonym of Margarita del Carmen Brannon Vega, was a Salvadoran poet who published nineteen books of poetry and a memoir. She met her first husband upon moving to the US in 1919, where she worked as a Spanish teacher at the Berlitz School in Brooklyn. They returned to El Salvador in 1927 and Lars received numerous awards for her poetry. She served as cultural attaché to the Embassy of El Salvador in Guatemala and later in the editorial department of the Ministry of Culture in Canada. Her best known collections include *School of Birds* (1955) and *About the Angel & Man* (1962).

Amy Lauren was a finalist for the 2019 Tennessee Williams Poetry Prize. Her chapbooks include *Prodigal*, *God With Us*, and *She/Her/Hers*. Her poems have appeared in publications such as *The Gay & Lesbian Review* with four Pushcart Prize nominations. A graduate of Mississippi College, she currently lives in Florida with her wife.

Molly Martin is an electrician, retired IBEW Local 6, and co-founder of Seattle Women in Trades, San Francisco WIT, Nontraditional Employment for Women, and Tradeswomen Inc. She is the author of *Hard-Hatted Women: Life on the Job* (Seal Press). Her short stories and essays have been published in many obscure journals and books. She led a group of volunteer tradeswomen to edit and publish *Tradeswomen Magazine* from 1981–1999. She lives in Santa Rosa, California with her wife Holly.

Jessica Lowell Mason is a Ph.D. student and teaching assistant in the Global Gender and Sexuality Studies Department at the University at Buffalo. A writer, educator, and performer, Jessica has worked for Shakespeare in Delaware Park, Ujima Theatre Co.,

Just Buffalo Literary Center, the Jewish Repertory Theatre, and Prometheus Books. She has taught writing courses at Buffalo State College, Carl Sandburg College, Spoon River College, and Western Illinois University. Some of her poems, articles, and reviews have been published by *Sinister Wisdom*, *Lambda Literary*, *Gender Focus*, *The Comstock Review*, *Diverse Voices Quarterly*, *Lavender Review*, *Wilde Magazine*, *IthacaLit*, *The Feminist Wire*, and *Praeger*. Her first full-length book of poetry, *Straight Jacket*, was published in 2019 by Finishing Line Press. She is the co-founder of Madwomen in the Attic, a feminist mental health literacy organization in Buffalo, NY.

Gabriela Mistral (1889–1957), literary pseudonym of Lucila Godoy Alcayaga, was a Chilean poet who won the Nobel Prize for Literature in 1945, becoming the first Latin American author to do so. Mistral was also a prose writer, educator, and administrator who actively campaigned for education reform in the Chilean educational system. She later lived abroad in Mexico, France, Italy, and the US, serving as a consul and teaching at various universities, including Columbia University, Middlebury College, Vassar College, and the University of Puerto Rico. She passed away in New York City at age sixty-seven and was survived by her partner, Doris Dana. Her best known collections of poems include *Sonnets de la muerte* (1914) and *Desolación* (1922).

Shelonda Montgomery holds a bachelor of arts degree in English with a creative writing concentration from Roosevelt University and a master of arts in English with a creative writing concentration from Southern New Hampshire University. Shelonda currently resides in Chicago with her son James, grandmother Emma, and nephew Justin. She is an avid animal lover and pet parent to multiple cats and dogs. Shelonda teaches English and Writing and mentors at a local community center; she also freelance writes. She wrote the original screenplay for the short film *9–5*, which premiered at the Gene Siskel Film Center in Chicago, and she was once a premier poet at the Black Women's Expo.

Samira Negrouche was born in 1980 in Algiers, where she still lives. She is a poet, translator, and doctor who has privileged her literary projects over the practice of medicine for several years. She has frequently collaborated with visual artists and musicians. Her books include: *A l'ombre de Grenade* (2003), *Le Jazz des oliviers* (2010), *Six arbres de fortune autour de ma baignoire* (2017), and *Quai 2/1* (2019), conceived as a joint literary/musical project with the violinist Marianne Piketty and the theorbist Bruno Helstroffer. Poems of hers, in Marilyn Hacker's translation, have appeared in journals including *Banipal*, *Pleiades*, *upstreet*, and *World Literature Today*, and online on *Words Without Borders* and *Arab Lit in Translation*. A bilingual book-length collection, *The Olive-Trees' Jazz and other poems*, will be published by Pleiades Press in 2020.

Natalie Eleanor Patterson is a half-Cuban femme lesbian poet from suburban Georgia currently pursuing her BA in English and creative writing at Salem College in Winston-Salem, NC, and working as a freelance editor. Her work has been published in *Incunabula* and *Neologism* and in 2018 she received the Katherine B. Rondthaler Award in Poetry. She often finds herself writing about the complexity of identity, love, family, and living in the South, among other things. Her chihuahua's name is Basil Pesto Panini. Find her on Twitter @natalieepatt.

Samantha Pious is the translator of *A Crown of Violets: Selected Poems of Renée Vivien* (Headmistress Press, 2017). Her poems and translations have appeared in *The Gay & Lesbian Review*, *Lavender Review*, *Mezzo Cammin*, and other publications. She holds a PhD in Comparative Literature from the University of Pennsylvania and is currently working as managing editor at Indolent Books.

Beth Brown Preston is a published poet, essayist, novelist, and memoirist with two previous poetry collections, *Light Years: 1973-1976* and *Satin Tunnels*. Her poetry has appeared or is forthcoming in the pages of the *African American Review, Callaloo, Goddard Review, Obsidian, Open Minds Quarterly, Painted Bride Quarterly, Pennsylvania Review, That Literary Review*, and other venues.

Sarah Pritchard, Pippi Longstocking-like, free-ranges with dog kid lurchers 'turnupstuffing' in the wild, UK. She's still personal & political & passionate about poetry strolls en plein air. Published anthologies: *Beyond Paradise, The West in Her eyes, Urban Poetry, Nailing the Colours, Manchester Poets Volume 3, Bang, Full Moon & Foxglove, Rain Dog, The Grapple Annual No.2, Stirred Zines, Picaroon's Deranged & Degenerate Voices on Domestic Violence, One Person's Trash. After The Flood* (a stormy swim through the 1953 floods of East Anglia) was a finalist in Local Gems Press's 2017 NaPoWriMo chapbook contest. Pritchard's second collection *When Women Fly* (the seven ages of a Mad Woman) was published in 2019 by Hidden Voice.

Margaret Randall is a feminist poet, writer, photographer, and social activist. Born in New York City, she moved to Mexico City in the '60s where she participated in the Mexican student movement of 1968 and cofounded and coedited the bilingual literary journal *El Corno Emplumando/The Plumed Horn*. She also lived in revolutionary Cuba in the '70s and the Nicaragua of the Sandinistas in the early '80s, and was ordered deported on her return to the US in 1984 under the McCarran-Walter Act of 1952 for political dissidence. She won her appeal in 1989 and currently lives with her wife, the painter Barbara Byers, in New Mexico. Her published works include over 150 books of poetry, prose, oral history, and memoir.

Robin Reagler is the author of *Teeth & Teeth* (Headmistress Press, 2018), winner of the Charlotte Mew Prize selected by Natalie Diaz, and *Dear Red Airplane* (Seven Kitchens Press, 2011, 2018). She is the Executive Director of Writers in the Schools (WITS) in Houston. She recently served as Chair of the AWP (Association of Writers & Writing Programs) Board of Trustees.

sb sōwbel's birth city straddles the Mason-Dixon line. This juncture is *The South* to friends in New England. And *The North* to Tio Benno (living in the north of South America) and his cousin, Uncle Ben (living in the south of North America). Solace lives in the liminal regions between. Heart companionship in the cold northeast and the sweltering southwest adds pleasure. Aiding adults to request college credit for learning acquired outside of academic settings adds the delights of service. Published works have appeared in journals and anthologies such as *Red Palm Review*, *13th Moon*, *Helicon Nine*, *Apocalypse*, *Black Buzzard Review*, *Bytchin'*, *Wormwood*, *InThe North to carnate Muse*, *Dakota House* and *Temenos*.

Olivia Swasey is a writer and poet from Cleveland, Ohio. A graduate of Kent State University, she holds a BA in English. Olivia is a passionate advocate for LGBT and women's rights and is active in her Jewish community. She has been previously published in *Luna Negra Magazine*, *Brainchild Magazine*, *Tablet*, and *The Esthetic Apostle* and has works forthcoming in *Breath & Shadow* and *Poetica Magazine's Mizmor Anthology*. She lives with her partner and their cat in Boston, Massachusetts.

Ashley Trebisacci is a writer, scholar, and higher education professional currently living in the Boston area. Her scholarly work has been featured in NPR and *The Journal of College Student Development*; this is her first published piece of creative nonfiction. Ashley's interests include: lesbians, learning, women's gymnastics, and a well-written college mission statement. You can follow her on Twitter at @ishmish17.

Jay Whittaker's debut poetry collection, *Wristwatch*, was Scottish Poetry Book of the Year in the 2018 Saltire Society Literary Awards. The judges wrote: "The unexpected vicissitudes of human life are grafted into the natural world—animate and inanimate—creating a deeply personal and moving collection. The poems are alert and humane, even humorous when least expected." Her poems have also been published in a wide range of magazines. She enjoys performing her work and has been well-received by audiences at the StAnza International Poetry Festival and other poetry and spoken word events across Scotland. www.jaywhittaker.uk

Joni Renee Whitworth is an artist and writer from rural Oregon. She has performed at The Moth, the Segerstrom Center for the Performing Arts, and the Museum of Contemporary Art alongside Marina Abramovic. She teaches poetry at the MacLaren Correctional Facility in Woodburn, Oregon, in partnership with the Morpheus Youth Project. Whitworth was the Spring 2019 Artist in Residence at Portland Parks and Recreation and Poet in Residence for Oregon State University's Trillium Project. Her writing explores themes of nature, future, family, and the neurodivergent body, and has appeared in *Lambda Literary*, *Oregon Humanities*, *Proximity Magazine*, *Seventeen Magazine*, *Eclectica*, *Pivot*, *SWWIM*, *Smeuse*, *Superstition Review*, *xoJane*, *Unearthed Literary Journal*, *Dime Show Review*, and *The Write Launch*.

Yvonne Zipter is the author of the full-length collection *The Patience of Metal* (a Lambda Literary Award Finalist) and the chapbook *Like Some Bookie God*. Her poems have appeared in numerous periodicals over the years, including *Poetry*, *Southern Humanities Review*, *Calyx*, *Crab Orchard Review*, *Sinister Wisdom*, *Metronome of Aptekarsky Ostrov* (Russia), *Bellingham Review*, and *Spoon River Poetry Review*, as well as in several anthologies. She is also the author of two nonfiction books: *Diamonds Are a Dyke's*

Best Friend and *Ransacking the Closet*. Her published poems are currently for sale in two poetry-vending machines in Chicago, from which the proceeds are donated to the nonprofit arts organization Arts Alive Chicago.

Notes for a Revolution: A Woman's Journal

A BLANK BOOK FOR WOMEN!

Order today!
$14 + $2.75 postage and handling
www.sinisterwisdom.org/revolution

The perfect gift for family and friends

Sinister Wisdom
A Multicultural Lesbian Literary & Art Journal

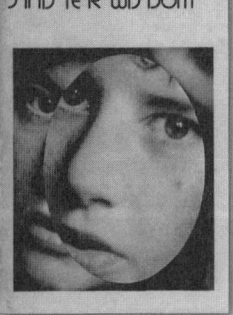

SUBSCRIBE TODAY!

Subscribe using the enclosed subscription card or online at
www.SinisterWisdom.org/subscribe using PayPal

Or send check or money order to
Sinister Wisdom - 2333 McIntosh Road, Dover, FL 33527-5980

Sinister Wisdom accepts gifts of all sizes to support the journal.

Sinister Wisdom is free on request to women in prisons and psychiatric institutions.

Back issues available!

Sinister Wisdom **Back Issues Available**

115 Lesbian Learning ($14)
114 A Generous Spirit ($18,95)
113 Radical Muses ($14)
112 Moon and Cormorant ($14)
111 Golden Mermaids ($14)
110 Legacies of Resistance: Dump Trump ($14)
108 For The Hard Ones.
 Para las duras ($18.95)
107 Black Lesbians—
 We Are the Revolution! ($14)
104 Lesbianima Rising: Lesbian-Feminist Arts in the South, 1974–96 ($12)
103 Celebrating the Michigan Womyn's Music Festival ($12)
102 The Complete Works of Pat Parker ($22.95) Special Limited edition hardcover($35)
98 Landykes of the South ($12)
96 What Can I Ask ($18.95)
93 Southern Lesbian-Feminist Herstory 1968–94 ($12)
91 Living as a Lesbian ($17.95)
88 Crime Against Nature ($17.95)
84 Time/Space
83 Identity and Desire
82 In Amerika They Call Us Dykes: Lesbian Lives in the 70s
81 Lesbian Poetry – When? And Now!
80 Willing Up and Keeling Over
77 Environmental Issues Lesbian Concerns
76 Open Issue
75 Lesbian Theories/Lesbian Controversies
73 The Art Issue
71 Open Issue
70 30th Anniversary Celebration
63 Lesbians and Nature
58 Open Issue
57 Healing
54 Lesbians & Religion
53 Old Dykes/Lesbians – Guest Edited by Lesbians Over 60
52 Allies Issue
51 New Lesbian Writing

50 Not the Ethics Issue
49 The Lesbian Body
48 Lesbian Resistance Including work by Dykes in Prison
47 Lesbians of Color: Tellin' It Like It 'Tis
46 Dyke Lives
45 Lesbians & Class (the first issue of a lesbian journal edited entirely by poverty and working class dykes)
43/44 15th Anniversary double-size (368 pgs) retrospective
39 Disability
36 Surviving Psychiatric Assault/ Creating emotional well being
34 Sci-Fi, Fantasy & Lesbian Visions
33 Wisdom
32 Open Issue

- Sister Love: The Letters of Audre Lorde and Pat Parker ($14.95)
- Lesbian Badge ($2.50)
- Lesbian Bomb Poster ($20)

Back issues are $6.00 unless noted plus $3.00 Shipping & Handling for 1st issue; $1.00 for each additional issue.
Order online at www.sinisterwisdom.org

Or mail check or money order to:
Sinister Wisdom
2333 McIntosh Road
Dover, FL 33527-5980